For Arthur Bielug
Love, Barb

Catina's Haircut

Terrace Books, a trade imprint of the University of Wisconsin Press,
takes its name from the Memorial Union Terrace, located at
the University of Wisconsin–Madison. Since its inception in 1907,
the Wisconsin Union has provided a venue for students, faculty, staff,
and alumni to debate art, music, politics, and the issues of the day.
It is a place where theater, music, drama, literature, dance, outdoor activities,
and major speakers are made available to the campus and the community.
To learn more about the Union, visit www.union.wisc.edu.

Catina's Haircut

A Novel

in Stories

Paola Corso

Terrace Books
A trade imprint of the University of Wisconsin Press

Publication of this volume has been made possible, in part,
through support from
the ANONYMOUS FUND
OF THE COLLEGE OF LETTERS AND SCIENCE
at the University of Wisconsin–Madison.

Terrace Books
A trade imprint of the University of Wisconsin Press
1930 Monroe Street, 3rd Floor
Madison, Wisconsin 53711-2059
uwpress.wisc.edu

3 Henrietta Street
London WCE 8LU, England
eurospanbookstore.com

1   3   5   4   2

Printed in the United States of America

Library of Congress Cataloging-in-Publication Data
Corso, Paola.
Catina's haircut: a novel in stories / Paola Corso.
p.   cm.
ISBN 978-0-299-24840-6 (cloth: alk. paper)
ISBN 978-0-299-24843-7 (e-book)
1. Italians—Pennsylvania—Pittsburgh—Fiction.
2. Immigrants—Pennsylvania—Pittsburgh—Fiction.
3. Pittsburgh (Pa.)—Fiction.
4. Calabria (Italy)—Fiction. I. Title.
PS3603.O778C38   2010
813'.6—dc22
2010011534

For
KURT VICKER
(1956–2010)
and his love of *la famiglia*

In ricordu di me nonni,
MARIANO CORSO E GRAZIA MARIA TERRANOVA
ca nasciru e moriru nta Calabria

in memory of
MY FATHER
and for
AUNT GRACE
who carried their names across the ocean

for my sons
GIONA DONATO MARIANO
and
MARIO CURRUCHICHE
who carry on

In the name of the Allegheny,
and of the Monongahela,
and of the Ohio. Amen.

Contents

Acknowledgments

My thanks to the editors of the following publications in which these stories, some in earlier versions, first appeared: "St. Odo's Curse" in *Long Story*; "Giorgio's Green Felt Hat" in *VIA: Voices in Italian Americana*; "Jesus behind Bars" in *U.S. Catholic*; "Catina's Haircut" in *Forkroads: A Journal of Ethnic-American Literature*; and "Mirage" in the anthologies *The Best Travel Stories of 2006* and *30 Days in Italy*.

For translating Italian words and phrases into Calabrese dialect, I thank Erminia Angilletta and the Calabria Exchange, Francesco Vollero of Locri, and Agatha Stellato of Calabrese Associates. Thanks also to Cathy Cerrone Fratto, who shared oral histories she conducted for the Heinz History Center's Italian American Collection in Pittsburgh. Some of the characters in these stories are inspired by them.

I want to acknowledge the *Valley News Dispatch* and the *Pittsburgh Post-Gazette* as sources of information on the 1936 flood, and my mother and Aunt Pearle for passing on newspaper articles and family anecdotes.

Mille grazie to family members Salverio and Domenica Campagna, who interpreted conversations I had with Calabrian relatives in San Procopio and Sinopoli that enabled me to learn the story of my great-grandparents.

I am grateful to my agent, Evan Marshall, and to my husband, Michael Winks, for their support.

Catina's Haircut

The Rise and Fall of
Antonio Del Negro

A story told and retold through the generations: father to daughter, grandfather to granddaughter and on to her children, each time changing details that portray the land—the worn face of Italy. Told and retold. But each time, the ending is the same.

Antonio Del Negro walked two and a half hours out of San Procopio and back looking for work. He gauged distance by the color of the earth. When it was a sheen of bright green spikes in the lowland, he was a long way from home. As grass began to thin and fade, he approached halfway on his return trip, and once the land had become a crust of gray at the base of a steep hill, the longest stretch of his journey home was behind him. Soon he would face Celina and what he must tell her.

San Procopio stood on a mountain of rock. After every rainy season, the soil eroded, exposing more. Farmers built half moon *lunitti* walls around trees to protect the soil from further erosion, but it was futile in this region of Calabria. On the days when Antonio was hopeful, he imagined that each stone was an egg of white and yoke that seeped into the earth and replenished it. When struck by heat

3

and weary, he saw one-legged chickens with no feathers, hopping out of cracked shells.

Today he was superstitious: he reached down and separated two stones, one on top of the other along his path, fearing he'd soon find three. But what was sure to multiply were the reasons he must give his wife to not lose faith in him, to not set her sights on the talk of revolution.

As he scaled the hill, Antonio turned around and eyed the plain below. Muddy coats of silt from overflowing mountain streams in the winter had fertilized it. Come summer, the valley would become a malaria-infested swamp, but this time of year, the lowland soil was drained. Earlier that day, he had reached down to scoop a handful. Moist, dark, and robust, it almost renewed his belief that if he walked far enough away from his rocky hill town, he could live off the land.

But Antonio's contract to farm a few hectares in the valley wasn't renewed. What he had to tell Celina was that he had no piece of paper from a property owner that named him a sharecropper.

He knew as well as the *patruni* that his shovels for hands and arms as stern as axle rods weren't enough. The proprietor sought a sharecropping family large enough to farm the land but without too many *vucchi inutili*, useless mouths to feed. Antonio was once blessed with five sons. Then his twins died in an epidemic. His two eldest left to find work in Switzerland. Both Antonio and Celina lost their parents in an earthquake that killed everyone attending Sunday Mass except for the priest who ducked under the oak altar as the church collapsed. This made an atheist out of Antonio, a man whose only dream for his youngest son was that he die a natural death in San Procopio.

At the top of the hill, Antonio faced a lone cypress tree behind his village wall, a mass of unruly stones built after Italy's unification. According to legend, the wall was never intended for defense. Proud San Procopians simply didn't want to give outsiders the impression they never had any good fortune to protect.

The sky's twilight was a slow burn to black. As Antonio walked through the archway, the faint sound of a bagpipe blew in the evening breeze. Villagers gathered under a lantern in the piazza to dance to a *zampogna* player who squeezed his instrument as if he were milking it. They kept beat to the music by clapping loose stones they picked up from underneath their feet.

The sound of stone, more stone. Antonio changed his direction. Rather than pass through the square, he chose a quiet mule path with grooves from carriages his father once told him dated back to the Roman Empire. He turned on a dirt road so narrow that he couldn't extend his arms without touching a doorway or window.

Antonio stopped to look down at his shoes. They were camouflaged by the dust and blended in with the road. That morning, he had polished the tips but not the heels, convinced that a man always makes an impression when he first approaches. By the time he turned to leave, judgment had already been passed. Now, he would face Celina's.

She waited outside for him on a narrow balcony where clusters of peppers were hung, the loose seeds inside rattling in the wind. She could tell by the way he dragged his feet that they were bubbling with blisters. *Because they refuse to form calluses*, she thought.

His weakness was her strength. Four years ago, when Italy entered the Great War in 1915, she led the attack on a soldier who was confiscating their grain to feed the army. She and a group of women stormed his loaded wagon, threw the sacks to the ground, and slit them open so they couldn't be lifted without spilling out. After the deed was done and he ran off, she told her husband that she would have defended herself with a farm tool. When he raised his voice in disbelief, she replied coldly, "If I had stabbed that soldier with my pick, wheat would have gushed out of his body. Not blood."

Celina, who even parted her hair off center, didn't believe in a middle ground. There was one side or the other. Strands swooped across her forehead, a black moon shadowing the white cotton cloth that covered her hair. She hadn't yet turned forty, but the lines under

5

her eyes were almost as dark as her brows. Droopy lids made her look tired, yet as soon as she uttered a word, they rose as if to reveal piercing weapons behind armor.

She peered beneath Antonio's hat. One side of his mustache was visibly wider than the other. He claimed he was farsighted, but Celina knew he intended to distinguish his broom from those of the other job-seeking *perdijornu*. This was his way of getting a second glance. Maybe the *patruni* would look Antonio in the eye, offer him work.

Celina shook a tablecloth, but very few crumbs flew into the air. "You left shortly after the cock's crow, Antonio."

"Prosciutto," he replied with a tired voice as he pushed down the sleeves of his muslin shirt. Out of habit he rolled them up to hide the holes on his elbows.

"Prosciutto?" Celina repeated, asking her disheveled husband what had happened. He didn't know she still received money from their sons in Switzerland, although he wrote and told them they were making do. She instructed them both before they left to disregard his letters on the matter.

"The man who got the contract presented a gift of dried ham. You know what I told the *patruni*? I held up my two hands and said, 'These are more valuable than the ass of a pig!'"

Antonio promised his wife that he would try another landowner tomorrow. Celina shook her head as she tossed the thin tablecloth to one side and began thrashing a quilt against the railing. Sternly, she said, "Maybe there is no tomorrow. Like today."

Antonio stared up at his wife. She stopped to brace her back, aching from the days she stooped to pick ripe olives off the ground. It wasn't like her to give in to *a fami*. Celina had *furberia*—the shrewdness of a fox. She had told her husband long ago that if he died first, she wouldn't wear black for years like most widows. Once she returned to her chores, she'd wear light clothes to repel the heat. "The sun has no mercy, Antonio. Why should I?"

He kicked off his shoes and tossed them at a lizard darting through the brush. "No tomorrow like today! My feet touch this earth, and your head is in the clouds, Celina. Never mind what anybody says. Talk. All talk."

San Procopio had four hundred villagers who congregated at church for morning prayers. They met in line at the post, awaiting letters with money from relatives who had emigrated abroad, and at the communal oven to bake festive honey biscuits shaped like fish, or their daily bread if their supply of wheat did not run out. As the bread rose, so did their voices. They gathered around the village well to fill jugs or strap barrels of water on either side of their donkeys and on the steps to embroider pillowcases for their daughters' trousseaux. Sitting together on door stoops, men carved *musulupare*, wooden molds that gave ricotta cheese as many crevices as a volcano, while their sons learned to work with wood by carving spoons.

While washing clothes at the fountain that morning, Celina had overheard men talking inside the *ritrovu* at the fork in the road. They usually had an espresso or glass of wine in their hands as they settled into their conversation. When she heard a cork pop and a vinegary smell drift out of the open green shutters of the café just above the fountain, she knew to listen carefully for news.

Although carrying wet laundry made the load twice as heavy on the return trip home, her spirit had been lifted that day. She had learned that the town's most devout Catholic, Peppina Santuzzo, had taken down a picture of the pope hanging above her bed and put one of Lenin in its place. Peppina's husband, Adelmo, even tied a red rug that she wove from remnants on her loom to the flagpole at town hall. "Now she prays for a revolution like the one in Russia instead of saying the rosary," Celina told Antonio. She too began to show her support for revolutionary land reform by wrapping a wide red ribbon around her head instead of a white cloth.

"We just got done fighting against Russia in the Great War. How could they be our ally?" Antonio said.

She told him how the men at the café said workers up North took control of the estates. Cattle were led to the stables and set on fire. "We can claim our land too," she said, lifting her eyebrows.

"But not keep it," he told his wife.

Antonio had reason to despair. Italy had been promised land after the war, and it was to be divided so that every man could support his family. Despite the fact that the war cost more than twice the amount Italy spent in all the years since it had become a country, the Treaty of London had been violated.

"We lost so many in battle and for what? We never got so much as a clump of dirt," he said. "Six hundred thousand men were killed, with room to bury each and every one, yet we have no land to plant life!"

Celina said there'd be land and they weren't going to settle for farming with primitive tools anymore either. They'd have *nmacchina* to do the work for them like the ones at the factories in Milano. And this thing called electricity where you could turn a light on and off through a wire. The way the men at the *ritrovu* were describing it, people gathered around a streetlamp to witness a miracle!

"There are no miracles, Celina."

She quickly folded the quilt and signaled for Antonio to come eat.

He entered the ground floor of their home where the farm animals were kept, a mule and a few goats. It smelled of damp hay. He pulled a few lemon peels out of his pocket and rubbed them on the straw sack where his son slept.

Antonio climbed the narrow steps up to the second floor, took off his vest and hat, and hung them on a hook along with his leather satchel. The room was dark from the smoke of the fireplace. At one end was a bed without a headboard. A gauze curtain of mosquito netting hung above it. Below the bed was a ceramic chamber pot. Beside it, a chair with a plaited straw seat. In the corner, a pine table with a water pitcher resting in a bowl and a linen cloth for bathing.

At the other end of the room, Antonio seated himself at the table as Celina served his meal—a bowl filled with *suppa*, the usual broth with fava beans. He looked at the color to see how runny it was. There was no golden cast of olive oil around the rim. There was no onion to flavor the soup, although she threw in chicory or other wild greens and mushrooms picked in the woods. On a plain white plate were a few figs glazed with their own juices. She lifted the lid of a deep trunk where she stored linens and dry goods, placing a quarter loaf of bread beside the fruit rather than his usual half.

"The price of bread went up again. I could not afford a second loaf," Celina said.

Antonio pounded his fist on his plate so hard it broke in two. "They just raised it! The *cittadini* are cornering the grain supply again to create shortages."

Celina gasped before she spoke. "There is a meeting at the *ritrovu* tonight. Socialists from the North will be there."

"As soon as they leave, the organization will crumble. Like the Popolare," he said.

Everyone in San Procopio had heard about the Popolare, the new Catholic political party. But there had been too much infighting between feuding priests from competing parishes. One wasn't willing to tolerate an action for which the other might receive credit from the Vatican, so the movement floundered.

"What makes you think they are any different? *Stranieri*," he muttered as he threw down his soup spoon and drank from the bowl.

"They are not all outsiders. Members of our provincial council will be there," she said.

"Show me a public official who refuses bribes and I will show you a white fly!"

"You will see for yourself how many people in this town wave the red flag."

Antonio dipped his bread into his soup bowl, then stopped. "What happens outside this family does not concern us," he said, chewing intermittently. He was no different from many peasants who believed they lost their say when they paid officials to resolve public matters.

"They will divide the property and give us all a plot. But we must join them!"

He broke off a corner of his bread and said, "The only land left is the Baron's."

"That is almost all the land," she scoffed, picking up the largest piece of the broken plate.

"You know they will not let this happen," Antonio said. "And even if it did, it would not be for long. We would have to start all over again. Maybe with less!"

Celina stood beside Antonio, clearing the table. "How could we have less than we have now?"

"We own land. What do you think this house rests on? This house is my estate! I inherited it! I own it!"

"The government cannot take it away from you," she said. "And if the Socialists win more seats . . ."

"No," he shook his head. "No."

She stopped cleaning when she saw his face grow pale. "Why not? Tell me."

"The government can do what it pleases."

"You are mistaken, Antonio. You said yourself, this house is yours."

Antonio lowered his head on the table.

She tapped him on the shoulder. "You are hiding something. Answer me. Answer me!"

He looked up and said, "I have no deed."

"How could that be? You own this house. You must have a deed—"

"Did you hear me?" he interrupted.

"No deed?" she asked in disbelief.

"I said no!"

Celina collapsed into a chair. She leaned her forehead on a clenched fist and bit her lip. "And you never told me?"

"I am telling you now."

She shook her head. Suddenly she screamed, "Before I married you!"

Staring into his soup bowl, he said, "My father was too proud to admit he could not write his name. And I was too proud to tell you."

"You lied to me, Antonio."

"And the revolutionaries lie to you! We are here by our good graces! And that is the way it must stay!"

"Even Don Marco is with the Socialists!"

"Then why do mules cultivate his vineyard instead of the men he used to hire?" Antonio asked. "That is ten people out of work. Don Marco speaks from his mouth! Not his heart!"

Celina jumped out of her chair. "It worked up North! It can work here!"

"When they ring the bell for revolution, we stay at home! There's work to be done right here," he said.

She turned and walked away. He followed close behind. They both stopped when they heard the sound of bleating sheep.

The rickety stairs shook as their eleven-year-old son slowly climbed them, pausing at each rung to catch his balance. Rather than continue, he stopped midway and shouted, "Mamà! Papà! Come down! Look what I brought you!"

A cart with wooden wheels was parked inside the double doors. The gaps were wide between the rough slats. Two sheep were standing in it.

Giorgino petted the fluff on one of the animal's ears. He was a gangly boy, wearing pants two sizes too big. He held them up with suspenders and rolled up the legs to the top of his boots. His jacket sleeves were short, exposing a shirt underneath. He wore his cap as far off his face as he could without it falling off.

"Where did you get the wagon?" Antonio asked as he and Celina climbed down the stairs. He was particularly curious since he had been forced to sell his recently.

"I made it. We can be vendors. Sell Mamà's ricotta cheese and figs to the *cittadini.*"

Antonio examined the cart closely. "Where did the wood come from?"

"Why, from a tree, Papà."

11

He walked toward his son. "Whose?"

Giorgino shrugged his shoulders.

"There are so few trees on this land that the owner will see it is gone," Antonio said.

Forests, which in ancient times covered the slopes, had been cut down to make way for railroads, farming, and herding. It wasn't unusual for the Calabrian landscape to have so few trees that one could count them on a single hand.

"I do not know, Papà."

"Speak up, son!"

"The tree above the stream. Giuseppe Punto says it belongs to him. Donna Maria claims it is hers, but her third cousin, Rudolfo, is convinced it is his and so is Don Angelo."

Antonio put his hands on his hips, arched his back, and began laughing. "The plot's been subdivided so many times they each probably own no more than a branch or two. And this is what your mother wants to fight for. A few limbs of a tree," he said.

It finally occurred to him to ask his son if he had chopped the tree down. Giorgino hadn't. It was struck by lightning and split into pieces that he could carry away.

"How did you learn to make a wagon?" Antonio asked.

Giorgino explained that he had volunteered to help the carpenter so he could watch how one was made. "He let me use his tools, Papà!"

"What makes you think you will not get caught?"

"Because Donna Maria accused Giuseppe and he accused Rudolfo, who believes it was Don Angelo and Don Angelo thinks Donna Maria's behind it. They already have enough guilty ones!"

Celina hugged Giorgino and said, "Divide and conquer."

"What he did was wrong, Celina," Antonio said.

"You know the tree would have rotted away long before they settled the argument," she answered.

"What about these sheep? Where did they come from?" Antonio asked his son.

"Signure Bullo is sick in bed. He asked me to herd his flock. In return he gave me two for milking."

Bullo had lost his sons to the same outbreak of smallpox that killed the Del Negro boys. Antonio had fetched a *magu*, but even the herbalist's special mixture didn't help. Within a week's time, four sons were lost to San Procopio. Because procreation was a matter of *onuri* for the man of the house, the death of a child, especially if he lost a son, meant that he also lost respect in the community that depended on the strength of the family.

"What about his daughters?" Antonio asked.

"They are not old enough yet."

"I see." Antonio was now smiling at his son.

Giorgino patted the sheep. "Would you like to meet them? I named this one Biancacina because it is white and this one Domenica since I think she was born on a Sunday. I'm going to milk them every day so Mamà can make ricotta cheese."

"How big is the flock?"

"Thirty. I have named half."

Antonio nodded, each time with more confirmation as he spoke. "You know, I think we will have enough cheese to fill that wagon. If the other merchants can make a living, so can we."

He eagerly began testing the joints and the wheels, and grew confident it would hold up with some reinforcement here and there. "We can sell our wares to the *cittadini* in Acquaro, where no other merchant travels because the road there is steep and rocky," Antonio said as he walked over to Giorgino and pulled his cap down over a crop of curly hair and boxy ears, which made him his father's son.

"I paid for the whole cap. Wear it all, Giorgino," he teased.

Celina shook her head and said, "Do not bother to name the sheep, son. You will just have to give them back to their owner."

"But I have to remember them all, Mamà, and they have to learn to come when I call their name!"

"Same as when a father calls for his son or a husband for his wife, she is to obey," Antonio said as he forcefully turned to Celina.

"Can I keep them, Papà?"

"Until Signure Bullo gets his health back." He reminded his son not to allow the sheep to nibble in the wheat fields in the plain or else he'd get in trouble with the owner.

"Those wheat fields should be ours," Celina said.

"Bring me the nails and hammer so I can fix this wagon," Antonio instructed his son.

Giorgino pulled two ceramic jars with lids from a shelf. He handed his father one.

Antonio shook the jar. "What is in this?"

"You asked for nails."

Antonio opened the lid and looked inside. "These are seeds. What are you going to do with them? Feed the animals?"

Giorgino shook his head. "Plant them."

"They are old. Throw them out," Antonio ordered.

"Someday everyone will have land. Give them to me," Celina said, grabbing the jar. "Get your father the nails and leave him to his work," she told her son.

Giorgino followed his mother to the small garden out back. It bordered a lemon grove. He liked watching the treetops above the stone wall shake as pickers climbed ladders high enough to fill their baskets. When he smelled a strong citrus aroma, he'd run to watch them pulp halves with one quick motion. The juice was poured into tanks and brought to a boil with powdered lime rock.

Their own garden was a couple of rows of tomatoes, peppers, and beans closely bunched together. Except for the lone fig tree.

Celina passed the jar off to Giorgino. "Hold on to them. For the day we own land," she whispered.

"What is it going to look like?"

Celina was astounded. "You cannot imagine it?" She seated Giorgino on a bench underneath a grapevine where the tendrils were coiled as tightly as Giorgino's curls. "Make a picture in your mind or else it will never come true," she told him.

He rested his cheek on the jar as if it were a pillow and he were about to dream in his sleep. He closed his eyes.

"Tell me what you see," she said.

"Which one do you want me to describe first, Mamà?"

Celina smiled. "You see two?"

"One is a wheat field with two rows and . . ."

"Is that all?"

"Well, there's a lemon grove and it has a couple of rows too!"

As much as Celina was disappointed in her son's vision, she knew it wasn't far from the truth. Most tracts were narrow strips divided from various farms, each in different locations.

"And golden wheat. The ground is covered with nuggets polished in the sun!" Giorgino added.

"You mean the wind from Africa will destroy our crop!"

"There is more," he said.

Celina stared at her son, who still had his eyes shut. She knew what was coming. If wind was the mother of Calabria, stone was the father. She folded her hands as if to brace herself. Her voice dropped. "I am listening."

"You will like this, Mamà. I see not one half moon on our land but fifty!"

"Fifty half-moons in the sky?" she asked.

"Around every tree," he answered.

"And do you see me and your father in the hot sun long enough to build fifty walls of stone?"

"They are already there," he insisted.

A sadness overcame Celina, as if she believed the moment her son opened his eyes, he would lose what was left of his innocence when he saw the expression on her face. She walked toward the barn. "Enough dreaming. We have chores to do."

Giorgino began sifting the seeds through his fingers in the open jar. He didn't stop to close it until the red ribbon wrapped around his mother's head disappeared into the darkness.

In the silent pitch of night, a bat flew through a hole in the roof of the Del Negro home where a tile had blown off. It hovered near the opening, one of its membranous wings fanning a midnight sky and one dipping below the bedroom ceiling as if it were floating on the threshold of time. Its shrill cries awoke Celina.

She lifted her head off her pillow and looked around the room through the sheer mosquito net around their bed. The airy curtain gave the illusion of a dream world where everyday objects were christened with a white aura—the water pitcher and bowl they used every morning to wash, the chair where they sat to lace up their boots, the terra-cotta oil lamp—all cast in a luminous glow except for the bat.

"Look." She tapped her husband's shoulder, then began kneading his arm. "Antonio, wake up."

He opened one eye and quickly shut it. "It will not hurt you," he mumbled.

"It brings a message for the revolution."

He took an impatient breath and exhaled. "And what about the army of ants marching along our floorboards? Are they part of the revolution too?"

"The bat is here for a reason," she insisted.

Finally, he opened both eyes before he spoke. "Yes. To remind me to replace the tile on the roof tomorrow."

"They want our blood," she said as he rolled over, taking the covers with him. "They want our blood."

Celina shut her eyes but couldn't fall back asleep—not even when the bat vanished from her sight. She couldn't stop picturing the span of its wings, which reminded her of the parasols the wives of the *patruni* carried to block the sun while the only protection peasant women had were the heavy water jugs they carried on their heads.

She got out of bed and walked down the ladder. She had the urge to see her son asleep below, to see his eyes closed off to the world around him, to the rusted farm tools, the bony mule, the half-filled barrels of rainwater. His feet were hanging off the edge of his sack, and the soles were blackened with dirt. She cried when she saw this and couldn't stop herself from climbing down, dipping a cloth in the rainwater to wash them clean.

The next morning, Celina's bloodshot eyes were as red as the ceramic tiles Antonio would use to patch the roof.

"Sit down for breakfast first," she said, guiding her husband to the table where she had set a small pitcher of goat's milk and a handful of hazelnuts beside a flat bread sweetened with honey.

Antonio was used to washing down a corner of bread with a few sips of wine. "But you made this for the festa," he said, slowly picking up the oversized biscuit.

"If we do not eat it, the mice will," she said, snapping it in two.

"And the milk? How will we make cheese?" Antonio asked.

"Giorgino can make cheese from the sheep's milk now."

Celina called her son to the table.

Giorgino eagerly eyed the festive offerings. He stuffed nuts inside the air pockets in his bread but waited for his father to take his first bite before he took his. There was an unspoken rule that since the patriarch of the family worked the hardest, he earned the right to eat first.

The three ate in silence as if words, no matter how few, must not break their communion. They passed around the pitcher of thick, warm milk. Celina handed it to Antonio. He took a few gulps and gave it back to her, but she offered it to Giorgino next. He drank a couple of sips, then returned it to his mother. As soon as she finished what was left and placed the pitcher back on the table, Antonio spoke with a force behind his voice that was like a gush of water.

"Giorgino, I need your help today on the roof."

"But who will take Signure Bullo's sheep out to pasture?"

"Do that later," Antonio told his son.

The boy pushed his cap down over his eyes and said solemnly, "Yes, Papà."

"Let him tend to his sheep. I will help you," Celina said.

"Yesterday you scolded the boy for giving them names because you said he would get too attached. Today you want him to disobey his father and herd them. A woman does not belong on a roof."

"I am not afraid like our son," she said softly.

Ever since Giorgino had fallen off a ladder picking figs when he was seven years old, he was afraid of heights. Even on the few steps to the second floor of their house, he grew anxious and short of breath.

"Today is the day he will overcome his fears," Antonio said.

He was firm with his son and seldom showed compassion or displayed affection, because he didn't want him to become soft. Not in a hard world. That was why Antonio would kiss his son goodnight only after he was sound asleep.

"Please, Antonio. Do you not see his hands are shaking?" Celina pleaded.

Embarrassed, Giorgino put them behind his back and bowed his head.

"He was born with two arms and two legs," Antonio said as he turned to Giorgino and asked, "Are you afraid to use them?"

"No," he answered without moving his lips.

Antonio walked closer to his son and placed his hand on the boy's body, trembling like a sheep that had ingested the poisons of white snakeroot. "Go," he finally said, removing it with a slapping motion.

Clouds of dust shadowed Giorgino as he herded Signure Bullo's flock out to pasture. The dark haze poised above made the animals' woolen coats appear whiter along with the oversized sheepskin vest of his neighbor's that hung to his shin.

"*Spetta*," he said, commanding the flock to wait while he removed a thistle from a lamb's hoof. The path this time of the year was a tangle of underbrush, and so Giorgino made frequent stops. He knew how vulnerable sheep were to infection.

He poured wine from a leather flask on the wound, the only disinfectant he had except for a lemon. While many a shepherd young or old would have drunk the wine himself, Giorgino knew citrus stung more.

"*Poverella* Biancacina," he said, tenderly petting the lamb. Unlike other shepherd boys who had no affection for their flocks because they disliked being separated from their siblings, Giorgino had no brothers and sisters in San Procopio. And his parents were so busy with their chores that there would have been no time for idle talk anyway if he had stayed in the village.

Antonio carried tiles out from the barn and stacked them at the foot of the ladder for his wife to hand to him. As he climbed a few rungs, she grabbed his foot. He paused to look down at Celina, who knew the Socialists were meeting and wanted to join them. For her, to climb that ladder was retreating from the land when they should fight to reclaim it.

"Hand them to me," he said, breaking free to scale the ladder. Celina followed him to the roof with a couple of tiles in her hand.

The aroma of pennyroyal was pleasing to Giorgino, for he knew that soon the path would be bordered with delicate ferns. He led the flock out of the woods to a small meadow overlooking a marshland of rush and reeds. Beyond was a calming sea.

Sheep bells sounded so sweet that it was as if they sprinkled the air with sugar. Even the sky seemed to open its mouth to let the crystal ringing melt in its vastness. Giorgino sat on the hillside and began whittling a tree branch. His father had showed him how to carve wooden spoons, but since he had watched a carpenter plane the wood for their wagon, he decided he was ready for a bigger project, one a shepherd would undertake to pass the hours in the fold. He would carve a crook that was as smooth as olive soap and etched with grape leaves on a vine whose tendrils climbed all the way up to the hook, which he'd sculpt into a cluster of plump grapes.

He made the first cut with his knife on the thickest part of the branch, the slivers shooting into the air like paper planes. He paused to watch them ride the breeze until he noticed the flock had wandered quite a distance toward a herd of goats near a rocky cliff side.

Giorgino ran, calling his sheep by name. A goatherd older than he hooked the goats with his staff as the animals began ramming their heads and locking horns. The sheep's whining cries were so high-pitched that Giorgino covered his ears as he approached, not knowing if their bleating was out of fear or if they were being charged.

The goatherd approached him. "Your sheep were grazing too far out. Vetch and clover are a goat's favorite browse."

"A sheep's is not dried up vine and thistle."

Pulling Giorgino's oversized vest, the goatherd said, "You are not a shepherd. You who try to fill in for a man much stronger than you."

"Signure Bullo is very ill," Giogino explained.

"He should have asked his daughters. They know their boundaries."

Giorgino gazed into the goatherd's eyes. "This is a common meadow."

"But I can draw a thicker shade from a tamarisk than you, and only I know where to find saucers of honeycomb and where the water rushing in the stream moves faster than a thirsty tongue. You should go back to the village where you belong," the goatherd said.

The noon bells from the campanile rang in a frenzy through the meadow and didn't stop after twelve rings.

Giorgino walked past the goatherd to tend to his flock. There he saw one of his sheep on the ground, bloodstained. He dropped to his knees and put his hands on her heart.

"Biancacina," he cried. "One of your bucks killed Biancacina!"

"To keep it from wandering too close to the cliff of rocks. A sacrifice you permitted with your roaming eye," the goatherd said.

The sky grew vague with wisps of gray that smelled of dreamy smoke rising. Giorgino carried Biancacina and retreated to another corner of the fold and resumed his whittling, but this time his knife gashed the meat of the wood. He couldn't stop staring at her carcass nor thinking about how the goatherd told him that he belonged in the village. It didn't help that his father had wanted him to stay and help fix the roof. He would have, had his mother not insisted she take his place.

He had been a coward for coming out, and now if he left, he would be a coward for going back. How would he explain that his lazy eye allowed one of his sheep to be killed, that he was carving a shepherd's crook? For that, his father would beat him until he bled.

His guilt drove him back to the village. He had prepared himself for the beating he deserved. He rounded up the flock and picked up Biancacina by her hooves as if she were on her way to slaughter, then stopped and carried her in his arms, leaving a trail of blood along the path to town. He heard what sounded like a pistol being fired into the sky. Giorgino dropped the sheep's carcass and ran.

As he got closer, he saw a man wearing a red handkerchief around his neck in the church tower ringing the bell and firing shots in the air. A band of people gathered and charged off with hoes and spades, carrying them as if they were weapons. They were Mamà's Socialists, he thought, calling for a revolution. Was she with them?

He scanned the crowd, then ran home. As he approached his house not far from the church, he saw bits of red tile shattered before him. The air was warm and smelled of blood. He stopped running when he spotted his father's hat. Then Giorgino turned the corner and saw the ladder on the ground, slowly following it with his eyes, rung by rung, until he saw his father's body lying beside it. He checked for bullet wounds. Papà had none. The shots must have startled him. He had lost his balance and fell off the roof to his death.

Giorgino threw himself to the ground and wept. He turned to look into his father's face, as calm as when he gave Giorgino kisses at night while his son pretended to be asleep.

Where was Mamà? He looked up and thought he saw her gauze sleeve dangling off the roof. "Mamà," he cried.

No, Mamà did not join the call. She was on the roof helping his papà when the Socialist in the bell tower aimlessly fired in their direction. She was standing where he should have been. He had been a coward, but his mother was fearless.

Curraggiu, he told himself. Courage.

He charged the ladder, grabbed a firm hold with both hands, and stepped onto the first rung. He looked up to the rooftop, grew dizzy, and fell.

"Mamà! Mamà!"

Giorgino ran to his neighbors for help, but nobody was out in their garden or balcony. He pounded on Agosto's and Fredo's doors. There was no answer. He pulled back shutters and peered into their windows. Nobody was home.

He looked in the distance for someone down the way, but it was quiet. The villagers had joined the uprising. All of them, it seemed, except for Signuri Valente, who sat on a chair in the doorway with needlepoint on her lap. He opened his mouth to call her but was ashamed at himself for even thinking to ask a frail old lady for help.

He ran back to the ladder. As afraid of heights as he was, he would climb up to his mother.

"I'm coming, Mamà! I'm coming!"

Giorgino removed his shepherd's vest before climbing the first step. He took a deep breath. He got to the second rung and exhaled before climbing another rung. His knees buckled. He stopped to steady himself. A rung, another rung. He glanced down at the ground below and grew short of breath. He thought of how his mother asked him to imagine the land they would some day own. Make a picture in your mind or else it will never come true, she had told him. A rung, another rung.

He shut his eyes and kept climbing higher up the ladder. He thought he heard her voice, *Tell me what you see.*

Giorgino kept his eyes closed as he spoke. "I have a picture in my mind, Mamà."

He climbed another rung and stopped.

Come, Giorgino. Come.

He lifted his leg to the next rung and pulled himself up.

"Are you there? I have a picture in my mind. Please, Mamà!

"I see wheat! The ground is covered with nuggets polished in the sun!" A rung, another rung.

Giorgino tightened his grip on the ladder with his left hand and let go with his right. He reached up for her, his hand quivering. She was still out of reach. He climbed to the next rung and reached again.

"Mamà! Can you hear me?!" His eyes were still closed, his hand groping to touch her arm. "Answer me, please!"

Tell me what you see, my son.

"Nuggets of wheat polished in the sun, Mamà."

Our land. You see our land.

He took three more steps to the top of the ladder. His hand found hers dangling off the roof. He held it, answering, "Yes! A field of golden wheat. That is what I see."

Giorgino opened his eyes. Celina was laying on the roof between a row of tiles, looking up into the sky, blood coming out both ears, where the revolutionary's bullet went through her. He gazed into her eyes and found life.

"I am here. Your Giorgino. I am here."

He stepped onto the roof and kneeled down beside her, gently dabbing the blood on her hair and ribbon before wrapping her head with the gauze shirt off his back. He propped her up on his lap and cradled her, so she could stare at the horizon in the distance.

"Tell me what you see," he whispered to her.

The look on her face told him that she saw their land pillowed in the air, warm and still, floating high above the cold surface of the ground. And just as he did on the roof that day, he stayed at his mother's bedside in the hours that followed, window open, so she could picture their plot of earth, there, everywhere, a vast shimmer of light.

St. Odo's Curse

Slipping her tiny hand into the mouth of a terra-cotta jar, Celestina Del Negro scooped a few olives for her father's lunch. She knew not to give him too many. The salt used to preserve them would make him thirsty.

To deliver his noon meal of bread, olives, and wine, she followed a path on the hillside, passing stumps of trees chopped down for firewood when they had become too parched to bear fruit, too parched for their withered leaves to cast an umbrella of shadow. The land in Calabria was so dry after another summer with no rain that its amber skin cracked into pieces, a mosaic of the sun. Some said the earth was on fire because *u suli* was so vain it scorched everything the color of gold so it could look down and see itself.

Celestina passed a goat with its head scouring the ground for a stubble of grass, though there was more bristle growing on the animal's chin than on the seared land. Cows pawed clods of dried earth, shaking their heads and snorting as the dust they loosened blew up their nostrils in the occasional wind. Their curves were no longer meaty bulges but protruding bone.

Crevices—wider than an arm's length and deeper than one man standing—divided the earth. Celestina's mother had warned both her and her older brother, Francesco Antonio, whom they called Coco, to watch where they walked, for fear they'd fall into one of the clefts in the earth. Celestina, a little girl of seven with rings of baby fat left around her wrists and ankles, spotted one ahead of her. She walked along the crack and spoke down to hear the echo. She discovered the voice from below was not her own.

"Who is there?" she called down.

"Is that you, Celestina?"

Her father had been walking to meet her partway for his lunch when a wave of heat split the earth from under his feet.

She peered into the darkness, recognizing her father's felt hat caught a few feet down.

"Papà!"

"*Piccirilla*! Find Agosto. Tell him to bring a long rope."

She dropped her father's lunch and ran back to their neighbor's house. His door was open. When Celestina saw that his sack for picking greens was not on the hook, she headed for the vineyard where she and Coco gathered wild chicory and sorb-thistle. She found Agosto raking around a knuckled root, sifting through a few strands of wild greens in the bedding. He was so short his rake was almost as tall as he was. A stubby, wooden pipe was clenched between his teeth.

"Agosto, the earth swallowed my papà whole!"

"Is he hurt?"

She shrugged her shoulders.

"How far down is he?"

"I did not see. Just his hat," she answered.

"What did he say, child?"

"To bring rope. Before he gets eaten!"

"The earth is as hungry and thirsty as we are," Agosto said, slinging the cord on his shoulder as they left.

These sudden openings in the ground happened frequently during summer months. The danger of falling in was so great that most San Procopians either carried a coil of rope or a stick to feel the ground ahead. The more cautious the pedestrian, the longer the stick, and those fearing *malocchiu* were likely to char the tip so as not to poke at an envious earth with anything remotely green. It was commonly believed that of all the ways to leave the world, by far the worst was to be buried alive, betrayed by your own motherland, devouring her own.

Agosto followed Celestina to the crevice and lowered the rope. "Giorgio, are you all right? Can you breathe?"

"I can smell your tobacco, that's how good I breathe."

"Grab the rope and wrap it around your wrists," Agosto instructed him.

"I cannot move."

Pulling the rope back up and looping it for Giorgio to put his wrists through, Agosto then tied the other end to Giorgio's donkey and handed Celestina the reins. Pieces of gritty earth began to shift in the hole as he and the beast tugged the rope. A groan was heard over sounds of stone scraping stone.

Giorgio emerged, holding his right leg as Agosto wrapped his arms around his chest and lifted him the rest of the way up. His muscles peeked through the tears in his shirt. His suspenders were as tight as mandolin strings, lifting his trousers high above his waistline. His pant legs hung just below his calves as if wishful thinking would have them wading in water.

Agosto smiled. "For once, I was taller than you."

Giorgio looked at him and said, "You are always taller than me, old man." Ever since Giorgio was a boy, Agosto had been a father to him since his parents were killed in a call for revolution.

"You are damn lucky. Old man Arpino fell into one of these traps and was buried alive. Nobody found him until it was too late," Agosto said.

Giorgio's clothes were powdered with dirt, his nose scraped and his forehead etched with scratches. Celestina patted the blood and sweat running down his face with the bottom of her dress as he reached for his lunch. She picked up the bread and put it to his mouth.

"My drink," he said. She tilted the jug for her father so the wine streaked down his throat.

Giorgio had broken his leg and bruised his knee. When Agosto helped him stand up, he whipped his neck back and howled.

"We need to get you to a doctor, Giorgio."

"It will heal in its own time."

"Ride your donkey home," Agosto said. "You cannot walk on your leg. Ride sidesaddle. I will give you a lift up."

"I have a half day of sunlight ahead of me."

"You cannot work the field!"

Agosto convinced him to go home but only after he tried to go back to work, hopping on one foot with his spade as a crutch until he ran out of wine to drink. Then he agreed to mount the donkey, groaning when they traveled along hilly, rocky stretches that were once streambeds.

Beside him, Celestina carried his jug in one hand and held on to her father's fingers in the other.

"*Muccarusu,*" he said, one of Giorgio's nicknames for his little girl.

He had a knack for giving his daughter endearing names, and she received them as if they were gifts. This was enough for Celestina to forget her father's misfortune until she looked up and realized he wasn't wearing his hat.

"Your hat fell off, Papà."

"*Domani.*"

"We can't wait until tomorrow. What if it gets eaten? It was your papà's."

"That bitter hat? Never."

Celestina giggled. It didn't matter what her father said. Just hearing his voice reassured her.

But she had reached down the crack with a hoe and fished out the hat. He was so proud of her, he let her wear it, and she reached up to touch its soft feather all the way home.

There, Giorgio made a splint from a branch Celestina found. She insisted that her brother whittle off the bark so the wood was smooth against her father's skin.

With the splint in place, Aida bandaged his leg with strips of muslin cloth. She never questioned her *testatosta* husband for being too stubborn to go to a doctor. They had no money to pay one. What she saved was for America. As soon as the swelling went down, the black and blue faded, and her husband could walk again, she would be satisfied that he was healed.

Celestina combed the brush for a walking stick to give to her papà. Aida was so superstitious that she singed the whole bottom half before handing it back to her daughter to give to him.

Giorgio dragged the stick and a chair out to the balcony, overlooking his crops in the distance.

"You would never know we have the law on our side," he complained to his wife. "The court rules in our favor and we still have to try and settle accounts with the owner. Nothing changes in this country."

Don Pasquale had requested a contribution of a dozen chickens per year to rent his property—despite the Minister of Agriculture's proclamation that produce be divided sixty/forty between the tenant farmer and the owner. And if tenant farmers like him demanded their legal share, they were arrested. By the time they were acquitted and released from jail, the landlords had brought in other men to pick the chickpeas and stack the grain.

"If only we were smart like the Germans, we would have collected animal piss in ditches and pumped it into the sprinkler system to water the fields. The grass would shoot up so tall and thick you could hardly cut it with your scythe," he said, thrashing the black iron railing with his stick.

"Come inside where it is cooler. Take your nap," Aida told her husband. "Your bed is ready."

Giorgio refused. He spent hours on the balcony, scouring rows of muted leaves for a sign of growth in the field before he turned his chair to face his house and the amber lizards camouflaged on the wall. He waited for the sun to catch the reflection of the reptiles' eyes and pointed to each with his walking stick.

Celestina watched her father from the canning area inside, stored with bottles of olive oil and wine, baskets of chestnuts, jars of peppers. He waved the branch about, whipping the air. She walked over to the balcony doorway, poked her head through the strands of beads, and whispered to herself, "Are you going to use it to walk again, Papà?"

She returned to the crevice the following day to get a better look at where her father fell. She stared at the fracture in the earth, imagining her father's broken leg as she ran her finger along the edge. It was a texture so coarse and fragile that clumps broke off with the touch of her hand.

With the twins sitting on her lap, Aida sent Celestina and Coco off to pick wild greens while their father rested his leg. She reminded them what to do.

"You go out walking and what you find, you pick." She pointed them in the right direction—to a farm with chicory or beetroot growing on its borders and a landowner who didn't cause a fuss when his property was trampled. Aida set out a sack for each.

Giorgio was adamant that this was only a temporary measure to hold the family over until he returned to the farm, but his wife knew better. Their plot of land was quite a distance from as much as a trickle of water. If Celestina listened with her ear to the ground, she thought she could hear the earth crackle the way her mother's bread crust did in the oven.

Before they left, she asked her older brother, "Coco, can we bring back some water for Papà's crops?"

"We need rain, so the streams flow again," he told her.

"Could Duce?"

"He doesn't have the power to do that, even if he just stood up to Hitler," Coco said.

"Then who does?"

"There are only two people in San Procopio who know anything about miracles. Father Orlando and Annunziata, the woman they say can brew magic."

"Who should we ask?"

Looking down at the long, empty sacks they each had to fill, Coco paused and then said, "Both. Father Orlando since he's a priest. Annunziata because she was born on this land."

The path to Annunziata's house wasn't far from the field they combed for wild greens. They approached the balcony where she was hanging clothes on a line. She was an elderly woman who had as many wrinkles on her face as the earth. She had wrapped a navy blue scarf around her head and wore a black dress and shawl. Her lips were tucked inside her mouth. She had one bottom tooth that jutted out from her gums like a chimney.

Celestina eagerly began speaking to the sorceress about her powers, but Annunziata waved a doily to signal them to wait until she came down from the balcony.

Annunziata tightened her apron as she spoke. "To start with, I will need holy water from three churches."

Coco turned to Celestina and said, "There is only one church in all of San Procopio. We will have to walk to Sant'Eufemia and Sinopoli for the other two."

"Plus a black hen and three yards of red ribbon."

Coco was stunned. "There is more!"

"Will a golden rooster and this do?" Celestina asked, pulling a ribbon out of her pocket. "My papà gave it to me. It was my nonna's." When the woman examined the stain on the ribbon, Celestina lifted her bag of greens and said, "How about these too? We can pick more. Fresh."

"Who is cursed? If it is a man, I must do more. I charge more. If it is a woman, I do less. I charge less."

"It is the earth! I want you to bring it rain for my papà."

Annunziata crowed when she heard this. "It has not rained in months! What makes you think I can change the weather?"

"You perform magic."

"On people, yes. I can cast any kind of spell I want if I set my mind to it. Princes and paupers alike. But nature, it has a will stronger than all of the people I have cured and cursed put together," she said, lifting her arms, her fringed shawl rising up like wings.

"Does this mean it will not rain the rest of the summer?" Celestina asked.

Annunziata chewed on her gums for a moment and said, pinching Celestina's cheek, "My child, this is not your worry. You are too young and tender to mind yourself with something as hardened as the earth. Is your father a farmer?"

Celestina nodded.

"Leave this to him," Annunziata said.

"My father hurt his leg and cannot work!"

"He fell in a crevice," Coco explained.

"What do you expect? The earth has the biggest mouth to feed," Annunziata said.

"Tell me if it will rain."

"Maybe a shower here and there, but that does more harm than good. What little water goes beneath the surface boils the roots, like a scalding hot caldron."

"She is right. Better to have no rain at all than just a little," Coco agreed.

Celestina frowned. "The earth tried to swallow him!"

"There is such a thing as too much rain, child. It is as much of a curse as not enough. Someday you will see for yourself." Annunziata bowed her head and said softly, "Whether you will it or not, you shall see."

Celestina sniffed back tears. "What about your powers?"

"I told you. I have no power over the weather."

Coco stepped forward. "Celestina! You heard the lady!"

"Nature is the higher power. I am at its mercy," Annunziata said.

"I have to do something for my papà, so his land will grow fields of wheat like his mother said. I am his *angelu custodi*!"

The old woman smiled. "Then here is what you must do."

She instructed them to drop a handful of flour in the biggest stream they could find and stir with the branch of a hazelnut tree.

"The mixture will produce a white mist and form a cloud that will rise high enough to be a fountain from the heavens. But you must keep your eyes on it and wait," Annunziata said.

Celestina offered the woman her sack, which she quickly refused.

"If you feed the earth, child, we all will have enough to eat," she said.

Celestina and Coco hurried back to their house, where Aida immediately divided up the greens.

Giorgio was sitting on the balcony, trying to read the letter his cousin sent from America.

"Has he found work?" Aida asked.

Giorgio nodded.

"Maybe he can help you?"

"Wait for winter," Giorgio told his wife.

"What good is that now? In America, it rains all year round."

"How do you know what goes on in America?" he asked.

"That is what your cousin says."

"Never mind what he says!" Giorgio snapped, shoving the letter in his trousers pocket. "We will find a way to collect the rain. Right here in Calabria!"

Celestina dipped into the sack of semolina flour and clenched the light yellow powder in her fist. Coco was outside searching for a hazelnut branch. When he called out that he had found one, they left for the only stream nearby with running water, Celestina with her fist resting in her pocket and Coco holding the twig up high as if it were a torch.

They climbed down the canyon of rocks to running water and got down on their knees. When she released the yellow-white powder, he stirred vigorously. As Annunziata had said, a mist formed.

Slowly, it rose, lifting the reflection of the water with it as if a mirror of light floated on a bed of linen. There was no way Coco could explain this to his sister other than to compare it to the Fata Morgana on the strait that separates Calabria from Sicily. The two cities on either side of the water are known to become one in a sea filled with the lights of both. The water disappears, and these cities feel so close, you are tempted to reach out to them with your hand.

"But we want water to appear like the land did for Papà's mother, not disappear," Celestina said.

"Then keep looking. Annunziata said we have to wait," her brother told her.

Celestina and Coco fixed their eyes on the mist and waited for it to change shape, for a rain cloud to form. For it to become something more than what it was. Neither said a word. Only when it grew very dark did they return home, still unable to speak, fearing words that expressed disappointment and doubt would break the spell. They couldn't answer their mother, who asked if they had picked greens. Or greet their father, who sat in a chair, bumping his strong leg against the wobbly one of the table.

Next, Celestina and Coco paid a visit to Father Orlando in the sacristy, being fitted for a new robe. He took off the purple satin garment over his head and handed it to a seamstress, who walked away with pins between her teeth. Celestina watched Father pull out a comb from his back pocket and touch up his hair in a mirror on the armoire door.

She walked slowly toward him, brushing her hand along the piles of embroidered cloth on a long table. She stood behind him and waited for the priest to acknowledge her. Without turning, he spoke: "Offerings in the vestibule."

"We do not have one," Celestina said.

"She means we already gave," Coco added.

Father Orlando turned around and said, "What can I do for you then?"

"We need rainfall for my papà's crops. I'm his *angelu custodi*."

"I see. A guardian angel. And your father is a landowner?"

"No. But he owns crops," Coco explained.

"On whose land?"

"Don Pasquale's. Then you will help us?" Celestina asked.

"You must learn to help yourselves. Open your Bible if you have one. Read the passages about the Great Flood and Noah's Ark if you know how. Go and pray that you are one of the blessed."

When Father Orlando saw that Celestina and Coco didn't move, he walked them to the door and said, "Look at them all."

Tenant farmers gathered outside the church, where they believed their collective plea for rain was louder and more likely to be heard.

Superstitions ran high during the dry season. When the weather was arid, it was customary for farmers to carry the statue of the Lord outside. During the winter months when there was too much rain, they rang the church bells to break the spell. Since it was a particularly dry summer, the parishioners asked to discontinue the church bells for fear they'd be sending mixed signals to the heavens. They would rather be tardy and have it rain than be on time in the midst of one of the most severe dry spells the town had known.

For every day there was no rain, they rode their donkeys to the church courtyard, circling the statue. Father Orlando frowned upon them bringing farm animals, whose dung around the base of the statue he had to clean. However, he stopped fretting when a *patruni* offered to buy it by the barrel to use for fertilizer.

"Your father must join them," he told Celestina and Coco. "On his donkey," he added.

She explained to the priest that her father hurt his leg; otherwise, he would congregate on the church steps outside too.

"Then take his place," the priest suggested.

"We need a miracle, Father," Celestina said.

"What do you think they are all praying for? See for yourself."

Celestina and Coco pushed to find a part of the statue to carry outdoors, fearing that only those who helped would be blessed with rain, that a rain cloud would form above some crops and not others. Since there was only one seven-foot statue and nearly fifty farmers, the Lord was carried horizontally so everyone could lend a hand.

Celestina touched Coco, who held on to the left ear of the statue. This was the best she could do as a little girl in the midst of a crowd of grown men towering over her. Dissatisfied with her position, she snuck under the statue and stretched her arms around the Lord's waist. She kept them there all the way down the aisle, the front steps, and into the courtyard beside the church. Now, she thought, if any rain clouds form in the sky, surely one will appear above Papà's crops.

While Celestina and Coco rode the donkey to the church the following day, they spotted a dandelion that sprang up between a crack in the earth. Celestina pulled at the reins, jumped off, and stood over the tiny flower.

"I am going to pick it for Papà," she said, hesitating to pull the dandelion out of the ground.

"Get the roots if you are going to pick it," Coco said.

Celestina took her boot off and tried digging around the flower with her heel but couldn't break the ground's surface. "It is too hard," she said.

Coco grew annoyed with his little sister. "Then leave it be!"

"It will make him happy to see something growing here."

The land Giorgio farmed resembled a tortoise shell long out of water with its muted pattern of hexagons cracking the earth. His crops drooped more every day. Except for a bright yellow flower. She wrapped her hand around the stem as close to the ground as she could and picked it. She climbed back on the donkey, and she and Coco rode to the church.

"Have mercy on us. Lord Jesus, give us this day our daily bread," farmers chanted.

Celestina and Coco took their turn on their donkey, circling the statue. As she passed its front, she held the flower under its nose.

With little to slake their thirst, donkeys began to tire out from the multiple journeys between church and field. Father Orlando blessed the sickly animals and reassured farmers that the Lord would look favorably on their sacrifice if they continued to pray and make offerings to the church.

But when one donkey collapsed as it circled the statue, the Northern priest discarded religious tradition. He resigned himself to trying what he had considered to be a superstitious southern folk remedy. He walked over to Celestina and Coco and said softly, "I am told by my loyal parishioners that to heal a sick animal, you must use the nightgown of a woman who has had twins. The ailment goes away if you rub the gown on the animal's legs. Would you bring me your mother's?"

When Celestina and Coco returned home to get it, Giorgio overheard them explaining the priest's request to Aida. It was then he learned of their visits to the church on his donkey and was so enraged he stood up on both legs for the first time in weeks.

"Starting now, that animal is going to work for me in the field. Not for that priest! He was not born on this land."

"You can walk again," Celestina said, hugging her father's legs and handing him the dandelion, limp and pale.

"Who is this for? The priest from the North?"

"I picked it for you! From your land."

"You should have left it in the ground where it belongs, Celestina," Giorgio said, limping over to his jug of wine.

"Where are you going?" Aida asked.

"Back to the land where I belong," he said, drinking half and handing the jug back to his daughter to refill before he left with his hoe.

Celestina tried to run after as he rode off on his donkey, but Aida warned her to leave him be.

"What are we going to tell Father Orlando, Coco?"

"The truth. Our father put his donkey back to work," he said.

"But when the rain comes, it will not fall on his crops."

"In America, they have big rivers, so wide and deep and long that no matter where you are, there is water. Even in the summer. Our *cuginu* lives in a city with three of them," Aida said.

Celestina's eyes brightened for a few seconds before she picked up the wilted dandelion.

Later, Celestina and her brother walked back to the church. Father Orlando was alone in the courtyard, smoking a cigarette.

"Where is the nightgown?" he asked.

"My mother said she would give it to you, but then she would have to sleep with nothing on," Coco said.

The priest choked on his cigarette fumes. "Then she must wear it."

"She says if you want to cure a sick animal, take it to the black-smith and have him wash its feet."

Father Orlando gave Coco a blank stare until he explained to the priest that the blacksmith must use a copper and honey solution and the animal will heal.

"We cannot come here anymore with our donkey," Celestina blurted out.

"Our father returned to the field with it," Coco said.

"But we want to pray for rain at home, Father Orlando," Celestina said.

"Is his leg healed?"

"Yes," Celestina said as Coco simultaneously said, "No."

Father Orlando flicked his cigarette ashes before he spoke. "Which one is it?"

"His leg is healed with wine," Celestina said.

"He is working but still in pain," Coco explained.

"But my papà does not want to go to America. His brothers are in Switzerland, and he does not want to go there either."

"Good heavens, no," the priest responded, stamping out his cigarette with the bottom of his polished shoe. He went inside the church and walked back out with a small, whittled statue, rough and splintered.

"St. Odo will answer your prayer for rain, Celestina, and yours alone. Do not tell anybody now. This is yours to keep. Just remember, out of the believer's heart flow rivers of living water," Father Orlando said.

Celestina prayed to St. Odo for rain the rest of the summer. Not a drop fell, but she kept her vigil just the same.

Giorgio continued to chisel away at the soil until October, when the rains came. Celestina propped her statue of St. Odo under the trunk of an olive tree. The first day it rained, she ran out and kissed the splintered statue. Her lips began to bleed, but a shower washed the red away.

Thousands of tiny pellets fell into mouths opened wide to taste the pure liquid down the well of their throats. Even the dullest, matted peasant's skin shimmered as if all the years of working in the harsh sun, all the worries of famine, were washed away in the shower. Aida cupped her hands and drank. Giorgio tilted his head so he could hear each drop of rain fall in his ear. Celestina and Coco touched the wet ground and waited for the soil to soften in their hands.

Celestina was eager to tell her father, "I prayed and prayed to St. Odo. He gave you rain, Papà!"

Aida grew solemn. "Our crops are still ruined. We needed rain months ago."

"I am thankful for it. Every drop," Giorgio said.

"Until there is too much of it."

"I will save as much as I need for next summer," he told his wife.

"The river dried up, Giorgio. What makes you think your barrels will not do the same? Like they do every year. We need a reserve. Every time they try to dig in the summer or fall, the ground's too hard, and if they wait until the winter or spring, it is too muddy."

Despite the rain, many of Giorgio's crops had been fried by the drought, and the beans that survived the weather were promised to the *patruni* for his pay in lieu of wheat that withered to dust on the stem.

Many a family had survived the summer months by stocking up on what they had managed to can in the winter. Aida asked Celestina and Coco to pick wild greens, especially since it was the season for fennel, asparagus, and cabbage.

Their father objected, saying they were scavengers on other people's property. He had rationalized that his failed crops had everything to do with his bad leg and not the drought. Aida paid him no mind. She handed Celestina and Coco each an empty sack every day when their father wasn't around to see. She canned half, including stems and root. The other half she sold, saving what she earned for the trip to America. And on the days that her children didn't gather greens, she woke them up in the middle of the night to hunt for snails. She instructed them to follow the smell of clover.

"What if we cannot smell it?" Celestina asked.

"Then listen for running water. Here," she said, shoving a bucket against Coco's side. "You will be happy when I make up a nice pot of snail stew."

Aida handed them sweaters, a lantern, and a crust of bread dipped in honey to eat on the way.

"Coco, why do snails only come out when it is damp?" Celestina asked as they groped through a field dimly lit by a thin, pale moon.

"They would sizzle in the heat and drought."

"Well, we should hide under a rock in the summer too."

"We do! By staying in our stone basements, where it is cooler.

Now start looking for snails crawling out of their shells. They are best when they have not eaten."

They followed the sweet cinnamon smell of clover to a pile of rocks under a bridge. Celestina held the lantern while Coco struggled to pull off a clump of snails.

They do not want to leave, Celestina thought to herself. Just like Papà.

Coco pried them off and filled his bucket.

As the sun raised its head above a pillow of clouds, Celestina and Coco returned home with five pounds of snails. They were bitter, but Aida knew what to do. She put them in a pot with a handful of bran and in a couple of days, they were sweet enough to eat.

During the rainy months, Celestina and Coco grew so accustomed to hunting snails and gathering greens that they could navigate the darkness as if it were daylight. And even though Giorgio insisted they would save plenty of water to last through the worst of droughts, Aida conserved nonetheless.

She filled a laundry tub up with water from one of the rain barrels, tossed the greens in, and began scrubbing dirt off the beet-root with a coarse brush. She pulled off yellow leaves and formed bunches. By the time the last green was washed, the water was brown. Sediment fell to the bottom while leaves and stems floated on the surface.

Only after she washed the last wild green to bundle and sell for the equivalent of three cents a bunch did she permit anyone to bathe. Each took their turn washing in the same tub of water, starting with the youngest.

If the water was exceptionally cold, she heated it over the fire for the twins, but by the time Celestina had her turn, it was lukewarm. She pleaded with her mother not to make her go in even as she slowly squatted down and was washed with a piece of cloth and a bar of olive oil soap. Celestina felt twigs scratch her ankles, beetles get caught between her toes, leaves stick to her skin. She imagined this is what it was like swimming in a river in America.

When it was Giorgio's turn to bathe, he refused. He looked into the water and said, "Those greens come cleaner than we do. Get a new tub of water, Aida. For me. There is plenty more where that came from."

She looked at him with surprise. "I was going to wash clothes."

"Scrub my back clean the way you do that beetroot! Rub my scalp like a head of cabbage! Wash my feet! Not some green!"

Giorgio led Aida to the barrel, but she hesitated to dip into it.

"We are going to need this for the crops, Giorgio."

"You do not need anything except me!"

She looked down at his bad leg and began to cry. "We will not make it through another drought."

"Stand by the barrel if you are going to cry like that. Save your tears for the summer," he said, waiting for her to crack a smile as he hugged her.

"It could stop raining tomorrow."

He broke his embrace and threw up his hands. "You worry too much, Aida."

"Then take us to America. Your *cuginu* can help you."

"I do not need America!" he said, raising his eyebrows, his forehead thick with wrinkles.

The thought of leaving Italy frightened Celestina. She ran outside to pray to her St. Odo statue for rain and looked for containers to collect water. When her mother was sweeping the porch, she snuck pots and bowls and placed them all around the statue. As her father slept, she added empty wine jugs. While Coco helped him in the field, she took his Sunday hat and turned it upside down. Then she cupped her own hands rather than fold them in prayer, waiting for St. Odo to fill them.

It rained for nearly a week straight, falling so hard it pinpricked the skin and so fast that the ground couldn't absorb it all. As the earth gave way, crops abruptly sank, disappearing in a swirl of brown quicksand. Those staying afloat rode a landslide down. Roots and all, they slid as far as a half mile from where they'd been planted, wreaking havoc with house foundations on the periphery.

Agosto banged on the Del Negros' door and stood there with drenched clothes, taking his pipe out to speak, so Giorgio knew that what he had to say was serious. "The Milotta vineyard is heading this direction! Coming down slow but it could pick up speed any minute."

"I doubt it will make it this far," Giorgio said.

He lifted his jug and offered his neighbor a sip of wine.

Agosto shook his head. "I will keep my eye out for it," he said, shutting the door behind him.

"We cannot stay, Giorgio!" Aida said, nursing the twins.

"Bolt the doors and close the shutters," he told her.

"Why are you so attached to this land? It is not even ours. You want to stay, go ahead! You stay yourself!"

"I support my family! I say when it is time to leave," Giorgio said.

"Not on this soil! It cannot even support itself let alone its people."

"This is good land. And we have had some good years," he insisted.

"In your mind, we have. Not mine," she said.

"Where did the money you save for America come from, if not from the earth?"

"From my will! And the grace of God!" Aida wasn't afraid to speak strong words to her husband with the twins in her bosom, when she wore their flesh and blood for armor. "You keep living a dream that we will own land, but we must start living the day," she said.

Giorgio looked at his babies and nodded before covering his face with tired hands. "I am my mother's son, and I am cursed."

"This country is cursed. Not you," she told her husband, for she knew that he could not separate his land from his own skin.

Agosto soon returned, carrying a sack of belongings on his

shoulder. This time, he didn't even have his pipe, so Giorgio knew something terrible had happened.

"My floor buckled. Wall collapsed. Door won't shut and roof about to cave in!"

Giorgio ordered his family to take shelter in the olive grove. As Aida grabbed a pouch of coins, Celestina bundled the twins in woolen blankets and Coco locked up the shutters. Giorgio and Agosto ran to get their mules.

They took turns climbing a ladder to a shelter Giorgio built on a sturdy tree branch. Aida went first. Coco handed her the babies one at a time. Next Celestina scaled the ladder and then Agosto, Coco, and finally Giorgio.

From the elevated view, they could see the hillside was a tangle of vines. Mud turned deep purple from crushed grapes. Fences were ripped out of the ground. Furniture dotted fields. The sky swirled with loose feathers from chickens fleeing their pens. The cemetery keeper's house was nearly a mile away from the gravestones. Farm wagons were nowhere near the farm.

"I saw it coming. The animals started to paw the floor. They knew something mighty powerful was underneath," Agosto said.

"Good thing you left when you did," Giorgio said, putting his arm around the old man.

Agosto, still breathing fast and heavy, shook his head in disbelief and said, "The Lord gave me a sign, but I did not want to see it. Plaster dropped from the ceiling last night. I thought I was dreaming of manna falling from the sky so I went back to sleep."

The rains fell and fell hard. Tree branches creaked and rocked as everyone huddled together under blankets.

The following day, a soothing sky filled in the gaps between the trees. The olives were thousands of glowing eyes, spirits watching from above, urging them that it was safe to climb down.

The earth had shifted so that its terrain was no longer recognizable—even for farmers like Giorgio who knew the contour of the land as well as the curves on his wife's body.

Agosto's house on the hillside leaned forward. The Del Negro's house not far away was untouched.

"The slide stopped outside our door close enough to knock. How can one house be blessed and another beside it damned?" Giorgio said.

Aida looked up to her husband and said, "Nobody is blessed in San Procopio. We are cursed, Giorgio. All of us."

Once again, the sun's rays struck the land like fiery arrows shot from a bow. It was as if the rain had never come and Celestina's prayers never answered. The statue of St. Odo was nowhere to be found. Celestina asked her father if he would carve her a new one. Despite pleas from Aida that her daughter didn't need to tempt fate with any more prayers, Giorgio picked up a piece of wood, pulled out his switchblade, and began whittling.

"The girl is just trying to help her papà," he told his wife.

"Then she will pray he takes his family to America."

Giorgio didn't look up, so Aida changed her point of attack. "And make us new walking sticks."

He rose in his chair. "Did you spot a crack in the land?"

"The floor is buckling right underneath our feet! I can feel it vibrate when I walk," she said.

He slouched back into his chair. "Give it time. It will settle into place again."

"The whole house is shifting! I am afraid in the middle of the night the roof is going to collapse on our heads!"

Aida hoped their house wouldn't pass inspection and the town council would evict them. She knew the only way Giorgio would leave was by force.

Agosto, who was barely recognizable without his straw hat and pipe, staggered in with a piece of paper shaking in his hands. "What does it say?" he asked Giorgio.

Giorgio took the paper and studied it. "Your house is not safe. You stay here, Agosto. Until we fix it up for you."

"He cannot move back in that house. It is about to collapse," Aida said. "And when it falls, it will fall on us. We all are in danger."

"Let the inspector decide," Giorgio told his wife.

Giorgio walked back to Agosto's to help him gather belongings. The floors were so slanted that all the furniture had slid down against the wall. Chairs on their backs. The bed tipped over. A table stacked on top.

Giorgio only planned to collect Agosto's hunting gear, a few farm tools, and bottles of wine that weren't broken, but Agosto didn't want to leave his bed behind. This was the bed in which he was born, like his father before him. It had a nest of birds painted on the tin headboard. Giorgio knew what it meant to Agosto, who had promised to hand it down to Giorgio and Coco after him. They carried it over to Giorgio's, where Agosto slept that night.

He curled up to the headboard and slept on the painted birds as if he were nesting with them. When Aida saw Agosto there on his pillow, his blanket wrapped around him, she thought to herself that at least one person would get a good night's sleep.

She stayed outside the covers fully clothed, lying on her back with a candle lit on the nightstand so she could watch the ceiling above her. She kept her boots, packed suitcase, and food for the twins on her side of the bed in case they had to make an emergency evacuation.

Aida listened for the tearing of wallpaper seams, the snapping of bamboo lining in the walls, and the splitting of woodwork around doorways and windows. She walked around with her candle and checked the floor and ceiling, and when her eyes were too exhausted to focus, she went back to bed.

Her husband fidgeted in his sleep. It was as though Giorgio's fears slipped outside his body when he wasn't awake to hold them in. His toes wiggled under the covers. His muscles flexed and eyes twitched as if in the back of his mind he shared his wife's fears.

Aida got up and walked to the front door. She pulled the handle, but it didn't open. She tugged, opening it part of the way. She lifted her nightgown and ran back to bed. "The door is jammed," she whispered to her husband, shaking his shoulder. When he didn't respond, Aida pulled at Giorgio's ears. He still didn't stir. "See for yourself," she said, slapping his cheeks.

Giorgio stumbled out of bed, still half-asleep, and pulled the handle. The door didn't budge.

"Yes, it is stuck," he said, returning to their bed.

Aida's hands covered her mouth. "How are we going to get out?"

"I will plane it tomorrow."

She shook her head. "I cannot live like this, Giorgio."

"You know we cannot leave Agosto here. He is a father to me."

"We will bring him to America with us."

"He will not leave San Procopio, and I cannot leave without him," he said.

Giorgio thought about sanding the door just to calm Aida down, but when he saw that he might have to remove it from its hinges, he told her he would do it first thing in the morning.

In Aida's nightmare, the doorway kept shrinking until it was so small nobody could get out. The same with the windows. One by one, the trim around them collapsed, and the glass shattered. Every opening in the house was reduced to a crack the width of a knife blade until it too disappeared, sealing off light and air from outside. There wasn't a way out of the suffocating darkness.

Aida woke up, screaming, her eyes locked on the door. Giorgio tried to get her to lie back down, but she just sat there on the bed, staring straight ahead at the door as if she were in a trance.

Shortly after sunrise, there was a knock. Giorgio opened the door as much as he could and peered out of the crack. A man holding out an envelope appeared. The shadow under the brim of his hat blackened every feature on his face except for a goatee and a small corner of his mouth that didn't move—even when he spoke.

"Are you Giorgio Del Negro?"

"What do you want?"

"I am sorry to have to tell you that this house is no longer safe. You must leave."

"Who are you?"

The inspector slipped a piece of paper through the doorway.

"What is wrong with this house?"

"Would you like me to read the letter?"

Giorgio snapped, "I know how to read!"

"Let the man in," Aida said, well aware that the door was jammed.

Giorgio's eyes skimmed the notice that he and his family were required to evacuate their home. It was in danger of being struck by Agosto's.

He threw the paper behind his back. "His house is made with bamboo and tin. Even if it did fall, it would not hurt ours."

"I am sorry, but you must leave."

Aida directed her response to Giorgio as much as she did to the inspector. "We have family in America."

"If we stay, will the town help repair the damages?" Giorgio asked.

The inspector shook his head apologetically. "The recorded damages are not considered to be in the public domain and therefore we cannot offer our services."

"Damn you, Fascisti! Where do I sign to appeal?"

Aida walked closer to the door. "How long will it take, inspector?"

"Eight to twelve weeks."

"Until then we stay here," Giorgio shouted.

Aida turned to the inspector, waiting for his response.

"I am afraid you must leave immediately. You have twenty-four hours."

"We have no choice, Giorgio," Aida said.

Once the inspector left, Aida quickly woke Celestina and Coco, ordering them to get dressed.

"When you are done, wake Agosto. We all have to get ready to leave," she told her daughter.

Celestina tapped Agosto's shoulders. When he didn't respond, she said, "He will not get up, Mamà."

"Leave him alone! We are not going anywhere," Giorgio stormed.

Aida picked up the eviction notice and put it in her pocket. "You heard the inspector."

"And you hear me. Let the old man sleep."

Celestina packed her clothes and went back to Agosto a few minutes later. She knocked on the headboard, then tapped him on the shoulder. "Papà, he will not wake up."

Giorgio walked over to Agosto's bed. He put his hand on Agosto's forehead. It was cold. He pulled down the covers and listened for a heartbeat, but the old man had died in his sleep. He continued to rest his head on Agosto's chest and began inhaling and exhaling heavily, wishing somehow that it was Agosto's breath he heard.

There, for the first time, Celestina saw her father cry. She ran to the crack in the door, fidgeting until she squeezed through to get the new St. Odo statue her father had whittled for her, hidden in the olive grove for safekeeping. Celestina prayed to it while Aida bathed and then dressed Agosto in his Sunday suit. She prayed while Coco built their neighbor a coffin, and before they closed the lid, Giorgio put Agosto's pipe with a fresh pouch of tobacco at his side. She prayed when her papà left to dig Agosto's grave.

She suggested they bury him in one of the deep crevices near Agosto's house, but Giorgio refused. "If I can turn the soil over for the patruni, I can turn it over for Agosto."

Aida began to pack. She wasn't certain they were going to America, but they had to go somewhere. Even Giorgio knew that.

She asked her daughter to bring her the trunk, which Celestina knew was swept away in the landslide after she put it outside to collect water.

She was quick to make her confession. "I put it outside to collect water. I did it for Papà."

"Did the landslide take your St. Odo statue too? Because we are done praying for rain, Celestina!"

Aida paused and then added calmly, "I sent your brother on an errand. I want you to take what he brings back to your father."

As soon as Coco returned, Aida gave her daughter the receipt for tickets to America and sent her to Giorgio. Celestina stumbled out the door along the path she had taken so many times to deliver her father's lunch.

The air was still and silent. She heard the gritty sound of pebbles scraping against her shoe with every step. She stopped when she spotted Giorgio sitting under a tree Agosto had planted as a boy. She came from behind him and covered his eyes with her hands, then showed him the receipt.

"Where did you get this?"

"Mamà asked me to give it to you," she answered.

"How did she get the money to pay for these?"

"I prayed to St. Odo for you and picked greens for her."

Giorgio stuffed the piece of paper in his shirt pocket.

"You like it better when I bring bread and wine, yes, Papà?"

"You want to go to America?" he asked his daughter.

"To a city with three rivers. One for the Father, one for the Son, and one for the Holy Ghost. Amen," she said, racing through the sign of the cross.

"One for breakfast, one for lunch, and one for dinner," he muttered.

Celestina looked up to him. "And when I say the father, I really mean you, Papà. You need a river more than God in heaven does. And a Fata Morgana so you will have land in the sky and on earth."

"Everything I need is here. On this land," he told his daughter.

"Why do you love San Procopio more than Mamà?"

"When I was a boy, my mother gave me a jar of seeds to plant on land that we could one day call our own."

"Did you?"

Giorgio sat Celestina on his lap and told her that his parents were killed during a call for revolution in the 1919 peasant revolt, and that the only way he could muster the courage to climb the ladder to the roof where his mother lay wounded was to close his eyes and imagine this plot of land that she hoped for.

"What does it look like?" she asked.

"Imagine you have a big jar of seeds. You plant them all, and each one grows until you have to look up to see how high."

"Where, Papà? I cannot see."

"There," he said, pointing all around them. "Everywhere."

Celestina turned until she made a full circle. She closed and opened her eyes quickly.

"You must give it more time than that," he said.

She dropped her head in shame. "Yes, Papà. I will," she promised her father.

"And if your papà stays in San Procopio?"

"Then Celestina stays in San Procopio."

"Your mother and brother and little sisters are all going to America."

Celestina's face clouded over before she burst into tears. "I will keep praying for rain."

"You would stay with me?" Giorgio asked.

Celestina nodded her head up and down as she showed him one of the water containers that she had begun to gather again since the landslide.

"Maybe someday I will save enough water for three rivers right here," Celestina said.

He glanced at the containers. They were caked with mud, cracked, dried out holes that reminded him of crevices in the earth, the gnawing pain in his leg, a season ahead where the air in the field would smell of salt from his sweat and not of Agosto's tobacco. A feeling of loss overcame him and he began to weep.

Giorgio stroked his daughter's hair and rested his chin on top of her head. He wept for himself, losing Agosto, then he wept for his San Procopio, about to lose him. "Tell your mother, we go to America."

Celestina hugged her father, but he pulled her away from him, saying, "Do not hug me, Celestina. Hug this tree. It is not going to America."

She scanned the pallid tree with its stiff, bare limbs. "It is dead, Papà."

Giorgio sent Celestina off and finished digging his neighbor's grave. He gazed at the curved imprints of his shovel scalloping the edges, the stones he raked to the sides, the mound he patted with his hands. Old man Agosto was the last thing he'd ever plant in his Calabria.

Hell and High Water

March 14, 1936

Mamà stares at the phone. She expects it to ring. Everyone in town waits to hear from Mrs. Marino because her house is closest to the river, and if she gets the water in her basement, it runs faster than you dial 2488W, our number on the telephone. I tell Mamà I wish we turn it off the way you do a spigot. But there is no stopping the river. It has a deep will and a wide way about it.

March 15, 1936

It rains again and melts the snow. Coco hears on the radio that the rivers rise nearly a foot an hour. I ask him if a Fata Morgana will rise too. He say no, just the water faster than the drip in our tub. And it is so small, Mamà will have to stop putting us in it two at a time like in San Procopio because there is not room for all the legs, growing long. The twins are still small, but she say to me and my brother in Italian, "Fold them up now. Fold. Fold." "I can't, Mamà, without snapping like a twig."

Hell and High Water

March 16, 1936

After school, I run way up the hill to see how high is the water. I cannot believe the river could be as swift as they say. But for three years since we come to America, I stop praying to St. Odo for rain, so I know all the water is not because of me. Thanks be to God.

Coco hears this is not the first time the river spill over. He say people read about an old letter from the captain in command at the fort where the rivers meet in Pittsburgh. And how the ditch the soldiers use as a cannon ball alley, a flood of water. People once sleep there and hide from the Indians. My brother tells me hell and high water go together like pasta and sugo.

That is all he need to say. We have pasta and sugo until Mamà runs out of canned tomatoes in the fruit cellar. When, I cannot say. She spices her sauce up with hot peppers so a little go a long way.

March 17, 1936

The phone rings. Mrs. Marino, she say the river turns color and looks for someplace to go. She has water and lots of it. They move everything they can to the second floor and go. She say workers leave the mine when water pours into the shaft. Water to the armpits before they climb a slope to safety.

I cannot sleep at night. I am afraid to wake up and find my head under water. In San Procopio there are groves with big olive trees to climb high but in America, no.

March 18, 1936

The river is all the way to the railroad tracks. The trolley in front of our house stops running. There is no school. Mamà say the Zeolla family will stay with us for some time because their home is flooded.

They are *cummari* and *cumpari*. That means me and my brother and the twins sleep in the attic so they have a room alone.

It reads in the paper the river reach 48 feet. Me and Coco go to the waterline and see firemen in hip boots. They row boats on Corbet Street. The water is some places 20 feet high. I can tell because the flag at the town building is almost under water. The firemen are going to rescue some workers when the flood surrounds the building. They come out and go in a rowboat three at a time.

So many people line up to see the rescue and cheer every time there is. Everyone looks very happy. You think a parade passes through town instead of the flood of water. I hear this man, talking about the river. "It's a rolling yellow tide, sweeping nothing but misery through here."

The man next to him agrees. "You wait and see. A typhoid epidemic'll come our way 'cause this river don't know when to stop."

They say how a gas line explodes, setting fire to a block of row houses and firemen have a difficult time to put out the flames. They have many buckets of water and still they cannot.

Red Cross workers in a big white motorboat desire to go somewhere in a hurry. The waves come crashing through windows and shatter into bits. Pieces of glass float on the river like the lily pad in a pond. Many things from the stores spill into the boiling flood.

"Look over there, Celestina," Coco shouts.

Three men cling to a leafless tree. Someone say their boat overturns while they try to rescue a family trapped in a flooded home. It looks like they sweep downstream until they grab the limb of a tree. I think they are very happy to touch bark. Like when we climb up our olive tree in San Procopio after the land slides.

The crowd sings "Row, row, row your boat" as many times as it takes for firemen to reach that tree. I forget how many.

Coco let me sit on his shoulders so I can see better.

"A hand in the water. Someone drowns," I say.

We run to a fireman as soon as we see. I tell him a woman with a red jacket floats down the river. The rowboat bumps into everything in the water. Each time, the boat points in the wrong direction, but I keep my eye on that woman so I do not lose her.

"She's dead," Coco say. "Stiff as can be."

"This way," I yell to the fireman and point. "This way!"

The boat rows near the body when the fireman reaches into the water and holds what Coco calls a mannequin from the department store.

Everyone at the waterline claps and cheers. The fireman looks more better now. Coco say he is certain it is another corpse washed up by the river.

At the moment, two men with no shoes finger banjos and accordions in the first floor of the empty building. They play "Sweet Georgia Brown" when they stop in the middle of the song. They pick up once they get to the second floor away from the water rising.

The fireman wades to shore and then falls. Coco and I pick him up and help him to the corner pharmacy. He say he works 24 hours with no food or sleep. He say the river is more powerful than we will know. It is strong to knock the Braeburn Alloy Company's brick building off its foundation. It crumbles in a heap. Whole houses go for a ride on this river. A person does not have the opportunity against a force this strong.

It is suppertime and dark. The firemen use lanterns at the waterline. Everywhere darkness except for the light of candles burning in the homes. A man sets up a stand on the sidewalk and sells them. Coco and I follow the trolley tracks home, stepping in the middle of the shiny black lines. Mamà asks where we go and Coco tells her the waterline. Then she asks what we do there.

"Helping." Coco speaks the only correct answer to her question.

"Stay out of the way. They have a job to do. And don't you dare go in that water. If you so much as get the bottom of your shoes wet, you will catch something from me that will put a whooping cough to shame," she scolds in Italian.

As soon as the Zeollas come, we eat supper. They bring the flood into the kitchen with their stories. Mr. Zeolla say 46 people die so far and 386 injured in this part of the state. He tells this story in Italian about him and his family:

"I woke up in the middle of the night to water creeping slowly up near the foot of our bed. I ran to the window and the whole street was filled with so much water. All I saw was a little bit of house across the way and men taking my neighbors from the window. I hollered to them. They did not hear. I hollered louder. They still did not hear me. I went and got the baby. Not a minute too soon because the floor gave and the plaster all go down and take the baby bed with it. I told her to hold round my wife's neck and I told my wife to hold round my neck, but I fell going down to the kitchen and my wife climbed back up the stairs with the baby. I was in water up to my shoulders.

"I tried to get some boards outside for my wife to float on. Then I got my foot caught in the fence. It was under water. I shouted for help. When I got my foot loose, I thought I was done for but made it to the garage. Men in boats came but would not take me. Said nobody but children were allowed and I told them to get my wife and baby. They took them and left.

"I stayed on the garage until they came back a long time later. All the time I was sitting on those shingles, I pray for my wife and baby and the lifesavers. I thought for sure we would never be alive. Where we go, I do not care. We are all together again."

As hungry as we are, everybody stops chewing the food while Mr. Zeolla tells his story. I think how lucky he and his wife and child are here with us now, even if they are going to eat Mamà's pasta and sugo more times than they want to count. I think of when Papà and I talk of three rivers before we travel to America. Never I think they can be like this.

Hell and High Water

March 19, 1936

Mamà sends Coco and me for water. The worker tells us to boil when we get home. There is also a place to get the emergency supplies—the food, the clothes, the medicine. Mamà say we have enough to go around. I correct. She says to me. Now Coco helps my English more and more. This is because he is my big brother.

"Nobody wants to hear it, Celestina, but it will rain tomorrow," Coco says to me while we stand in the water line.

"Then keep the voice down," I whisper.

In some places where the water is less, people move out boxes of things they own. Men line up with something heavy on their shoulders. The way they carry, I believe they are coffins. Coco said this is true.

A man at the water hole says how the morgue must buy 300 yards of muslin to cover all the bodies in long rows.

March 20, 1936

Coco takes me to a cliff near the Tarentum Bridge, where we watch the river.

"A piano!" I shout.

Some man, who is leaving his place along the ledge, says, "Look for the Schenley whiskey barrels. The company'll pay good money for those."

"I see a bushel of apples. Let's get," I tell my brother.

"We can't do that. The river's diseased with typhoid. If I were going to jump in, I wouldn't chase down no apples. I could sell the whiskey on the street and get my price, being they closed down all the state stores," he says.

Besides the apples and the piano, he and I find many things in the river—baby dolls, go-carts, oil tanks. Even a roll-top desk we understand is used as a life raft.

I think what it will be like to swim in the river with everything in it. It is brown and too much. I understand what Annunziata once tell me and my big brother. In San Procopio and in America, sometimes there is too much.

March 21, 1936

Yellow-brown ooze sticks to everything. Sidewalks are lined with furniture, all of it covered with mud. Coco and I see people on the streets. First with shovels and brooms and then mops to clean away the mud. One woman sits in a chair to scrub her bed before she throws buckets of water over it. Another woman cries as she opens up her hope chest to find the lace linen coated with mud.

Mud fills pots and pans, radios, washing machines, refrigerators, cupboards, even pianos. Mud a foot to six feet deep in some places. Walls sag from mud and buildings lean at crazy angles from the force of the river. It reminds me of Agosto's house in San Procopio.

And when Coco and I get shovels to help dig up the mud, I think of Papà digging his grave. How he plant him like a seed.

As we scoop up the piles of mud, a man runs down the street with a broom high in the air. He heads to the waterline.

"Now listen Miss Allegheny, why don't you go along about your business? I ain't botherin' you none at all. I ain't even askin' you t'help me put up this here shack I'm buildin' to replace the one you took down to Wheeling with you last week," he said as the river lapped the shore another inch higher.

"I'm tellin' you, lady, you know how I come along last year and fixed up a place here. Brang my wife, Mary, my little boy, Howie, and my daughter, Shirley, just born."

The river licked up a little more. "And I build her back again, remember. I bring stuffin' for the cracks, a stove from the dump, and me and the kids is snug. We was nice to you, Missus. We took all the rubbish way out to the dump, and we throwed no morsel in you.

"The wife, she comes back from the church St. Patrick's night.

We have some food and out there you're actin' fierce. The rain rattled on the ruff, that night, and you come right over the slab I fixed by the door."

A boat goes by and waves roll over the man's foot. He hurries ankle deep into the river and shakes his broom at the waters.

"I tell you, Miss Allegheny, you're goin' just a little too damned far! I didn't say a single bad word when you chased us all out of our house. I come back here quiet and started to build me another place. But you don't know no shame."

Coco and I get out of the man's way and walk over to a sign with names of the homeless.

"I bet there's at least a thousand names on this piece of paper," my brother says.

I like to argue with him because a younger sister has no choice but to stand up to her big brother, but this time I believe him. This makes me want to find the good in the river.

"I know where we can get the hip boots—the kind fishermen wear in the river," I tell Coco.

I show him a pile of boots. We slip the rubbery things on and begin the walk up the street. The mud is a thick batter as we head to our church to see if we can pray there on Sunday. We walk up the main aisle to the sanctuary, the holiest place in the church. The river is there. The big cross above the altar is upside down. It looks like Jesus is hanging by his toes. And the big statue of the Blessed Mother is face down on the muddy altar.

I wonder what kind of penance the river will get. More Hail Marys than I can count or maybe the priest will not forgive. I wonder if the river can save its soul. I put all my faith in it. In San Procopio, I pray for an America with three rivers, one for the Father, the Son, and the Holy Ghost. But Papà does not need the river to water his crops. He is not a farmer anymore. He is what they call a landscaper. He cuts and prunes the shrubs around big houses up the hill. He plants trees that don't bear fruit and rose bushes. And very soon, he may not plant anything at all to take work in a plant that makes steel or glass or concrete. I ask Coco why they call it a plant when it does not grow food for the family. This is the wrong kind of plant for Papà, I tell him. And why is it near the river?

Maybe I think the river is a place to swim and go in it more than I go to church. I will feel clean after washing myself in the waters and dirty after Mass where I must remember all my sins. But now I do not know what to think.

"Can we stand the statue up?" I ask Coco.

When we do, we find there is nothing but a big hole where the face of the Blessed Mother should be. It is in pieces on the altar. We move it to a place that is not so muddy. We carry it on its side like we carry the statue of the Lord in San Procopio, so everyone can touch and be blessed if he give us rain. But this statue cannot bless. I run out of the church so my brother will not see me cry. He comes out and says it isn't my fault.

We are about to head back when Coco calls out, "This way! I hear somebody crying!"

We walk through deep mud closer to the waterline.

"It's coming from there!" He points to a two-story house resting on its side.

The mud is very wet and slippery. People talk about a lady with child trapped in her burning home and the firemen have trouble getting to her. They try to climb a big beam to the top of the house where she is but slide down because it is covered in mud.

Soon after that, they tell the woman to sit on the beam and go down like a sliding board. There is so much mud, she goes straight down and lands in a rescue boat.

Two firemen catch the woman and set her down very easy. She rests her head on the fireman's lap and begins to scream and hold her big belly. A Red Cross nurse reaches under her dress and pulls out a baby!

I am so happy for the mud, I lower the rest of my body in it before standing back up. It feels good and when Mamà scolds me, I think it will feel even better.

Hell and High Water

March 22, 1936

Rain and fog set in. People put their brooms and shovels down and let the downpour clean off the mud for them. It is just enough to bring everything out again. Colors and textures and shapes under brown reappear.

March 23, 1936

I know things are getting better when the milkman delivers again. It won't be long before Coco and I have to go back to school. Now I have many pages of my journal to show my teacher, how each day I practice my English, and each day I get better. That and Coco telling me what to write. My brother says we write enough. He asks me if I want to spend another day at the waterline, but I don't want to go this time. Besides, Mamà is punishing me for the mud on my clothes and in my hair, inside my ears and caked on my eyelashes.

Mamà said I am to watch the Zeolla's baby Mima while they go back to their apartment to see what is left. I keep thinking about that baby born in the mud. I guess Mima sees the smile on my face. She stops her pouting, and like the river, reflects my grin on back to me.

Giorgio's Green Felt Hat

The river was muddy, the color of sun-baked earth, and the hat floated on its murky waters. It was the hat my grandfather wore the day he came to this country, and only when it was drowning in the river's bliss did I believe that if I could rescue it—if I could somehow swim across the amber stream and hold it in my hands—I could save my grandfather's life.

The day his hat dove into the river, I was ten years old. He and I had taken our usual stroll past the cannon in Riverview Park. He hobbled and I ran ahead to slide down its barrel as if it were a banister.

He watched, stretching out his arms the size of a bushel basket ready to catch me. I couldn't see him, just the feather sprouting out of his hat, and it made me ticklish under my chin.

I told him this was no different than climbing a limb of a tree, and I had climbed the willow behind our house at least a hundred times. He nodded his head but his arms didn't budge.

After that, we sat on the park bench and watched the boats go by on the Allegheny. I looked for the speedboats, especially the ones with water skiers, so I could see their trails mark up the river like chalk on a blackboard. My grandfather eyed the tugboats. He liked them best because they were slow. Said you could watch them longer.

"See that gravel," he said, pointing to the mountain of dusty gray on one of the barges. "I made steps and sidewalks and driveways with that. Foundations too."

He was trying to smile about all that concrete because it was how he came to make a living until he retired. But I could see him looking down at the grass, patting it with his foot, and knew he had to be thinking if only there were less concrete, there might be more land for food.

My grandfather was a farmer from Calabria. When he came to this country in 1934, he wished he could have taken a patch of land with him. I saw a photo of the day he arrived with my mother and the rest of the family and was convinced his fingernails were black moons from the soil of his homeland, because it was the only way he could bring it to America.

He was wearing his hat that day. It was shaped like a hill town, and the feather at the top stood like a lone cypress. Its felt, once smooth and green, had turned brown from the sun sucking it dry all the years he worked the land in San Procopio. It was the hat his father wore to his dying day, the hat my mother found in a crevice he once fell in.

He wore it in our Pittsburgh river town as he did back in San Procopio, and all the curious stares at him slid right off the slope of his curly brim. My nonna said he'd wear that hat in the shower if he could figure out a way it wouldn't get wet. Said that would be the best thing that could happen to it, because that hat of his could use a heavy soaking it was so faded and weather-beaten. She was always trying to get him to take it off, because she said it made him look like a peasant, and yet that's why my grandfather liked it so much. Because he would never be mistaken for a *patruni* in that hat. I didn't say anything, but I thought Nonna was right.

"You can't grow a fig tree in a bucket of cement," he said, as the tugboat pushed the barge forward.

I could just hear Nonna now, saying the land in San Procopio was so hard and dry it might as well have been cement.

I had this hunch he knew he was paid all those years to do the wrong thing when he came to this country. Instead of burying soil under those thick slabs, he should have been tearing them up so the earth could breathe again and be nourished by the rain and the sun spooning rays in each and every hole in the ground like it were a mouth to feed. When I asked him about it, he said even concrete couldn't stop some things from growing. He smiled when he said it too. Told me that's how come dandelions spring up from the cracks, how my mother plucked one from the hard earth in San Procopio for him once.

"Don't matter where they grow from," he said. "I can fry those up 'til they're nice and tender. Dandelions are good to me, so they are."

When he lived in San Procopio, he told me he ate off the land. Maybe Nonna would say they didn't eat enough and were hungry. But Nonno saw it another way. He said he didn't have to go to the Acme supermarket like he does now. What he didn't grow, he traded with his neighbors. This way everybody in town had what they needed. I asked him how come he came to this country if he didn't like to go grocery shopping. He told me this story:

"I farmed land in San Procopio so rich and fertile, when I combed my hands through the earth, it was as soft as brown sugar in the best of seasons. In the valley and along the hillside, fig trees and olive orchards and vineyards grew. Almonds and chestnuts. Every fruit and vegetable.

"We ate good and lived good on our little mountain. And in the right time of the year, it was as green as old man Agosto could make it. He was the best farmer in all of San Procopio. How he harvested with his sickle. Problem was the season didn't last. There were dry spells and cracks in the earth big enough for a man my size to fall in. Can you imagine that, Celeste? Hat and all!

"But one day, after your mother and Uncle Coco prayed and prayed, rain fell from the sky to make up for all the while it never did. Pretty soon, our land was buried in mud, and we stayed in an olive tree until the landslides stopped and we could farm again.

"Soon enough, the soil became as dry and hard as concrete once more. I got down on my knees and put my hand on the crusty earth, and it was skin and bone. Skin and bone. How could it feed me when it was starving to death?

"Then the time came for more prayers and more rain to fall, but the next landslide was swifter than the one before. It was so strong that it swept away houses and grapevines, cattle and wheat fields, so strong that it took away a man's will to live, a man who spent a lifetime living off the land, living through the seasons. Old man Agosto, a man who was a father to me when my own father and mother had died. And the day I buried him was the day I knew I'd have to leave the old country behind, because without him our hill town would never turn green again."

"How about a Fata Morgana that my mother talks of? Will the sky turn into one again someday?"

He smiled and told me the same story he had told my mother about his parents being killed during a call for revolution in San Procopio. "The last thing my mother saw before she died was her land floating in the sky."

"Did she look hard?"

"All her life."

"Did you see it too, Nonno?"

"When I closed my eyes, I could picture what she saw."

"How about Mamà? Can she?"

"You'll have to ask her," he said.

My grandfather jingled the change in his pocket, which meant it was time to toss a few pennies in the water fountain and count the fish instead of the coins, because there weren't as many. He made me count in Italian, and that language seemed as slippery on my tongue as I imagined those fish would be in my hands. I remember asking him why we couldn't see any fish swimming in the river, and he said the river was too deep.

"How deep?"

"You know what comes after *dieci* in Italian?" he asked.

"*Vinti, trenta, quaranta, cinquanta, settanta, ottanta, novanta,*" I belted out. Then I inhaled and decided that counting in Italian is like reaching the bottom of the river. You can't do it in one breath.

He pulled out the bag of breadcrumbs to toss to the ducks. Each was a little victory because Nonna said they would make a perfect stuffing for her artichokes. She started out giving us less than a handful. I heard him tell her she used bigger pinches of salt than that when she cooked, so she tossed a few more crumbs in the bag and told him to go stuff them in his hat.

We went back up the hill to the park bench and waited for another boat to pass. We didn't see any under the bridge, so Nonno shifted to face the other direction. This way he could follow the tugboat and a machine claw into the river to scoop up gravel. His arms were stretched out on the top of the park bench, motionless as if they were nailed there. I was peeking through the opening between the bench slats when his hat flew into the air.

I ran after it as he jumped out of his seat. A minute ago, it was so near that I could see the thin, matted fibers growing from the belly of the hat. Now it drifted toward the river below and got caught in a bed of purple morning glories along the cliff.

He followed it to the slope and opened his legs wide like a stepladder, which took some doing with his bad knee. He reached as far as he could but was inches shy. I asked him to hold my arm while I climbed down to get it, but when I got my fingers on the rim of the hat, it tipped over and tumbled down. I couldn't help but think how happy Nonna would be if he lost it.

We took the stairs to the dock, Nonno holding on to me and the railing. The wooden steps creaked and shook as we made our way, and I got my foot caught in a big knothole in a board on the landing. My grandfather yanked my foot out like it was one of his dandelions. There was a rope for a railing and he made me hold on to it. I burned the inside of my hand brushing against it because I held on so tight and ran down so fast, but the hat darted right past us into the water.

The wind had taken a backseat in the sky. The hat seemed to dive on its own free will, tucking itself between two voluptuous waves the way a baby rests its head in a mother's bosom. At that moment, it was as though his hat claimed a life of its own. Or so I hoped, because I began to wonder if it were my fault, that I somehow wished the hat away.

"My hat! My hat!" he yelled, running to the riverbank as fast as he could with a knee he couldn't fully bend.

I thought about putting my hand in the water, but I was afraid. Afraid of what might be underneath. He tried to snag it with a long branch, but instead it moved a little farther out from the bank. I thought I could see the fuzz on the hat grow like moss, thicker and thicker.

"Look how fast it's going! Right by us," I said, ready to watch it disappear.

I looked over at my grandfather. His eyes were watering up. At first I thought it was the reflection from the river. Then I knew better. He was attached to that old felt hat as much as I was to a stuffed monkey I had had growing up. I couldn't get to sleep at night unless I tucked my hand underneath his suspenders. In fact, I couldn't do much of anything without him, and my mother knew better than to even suggest I pass it on to my younger brother.

"I know how to swim. I'll get it for you, Nonno. It's just water," I said to make him feel better and me too. But there was no way of knowing what we couldn't see. Even the sun knocking hard couldn't get through the river's muddy surface.

My grandfather paced a few times, thinking what to do next. He grabbed a rope from the dock and hurled it toward the hat. It smacked on the water and sent the hat a little bit farther away from the bank. As it floated out, the water seemed to kick in a swirl and stopped being so muddy.

"Let me go in, Nonno! I know how to swim!"

He grabbed the branch again and tried to fish his hat out of the water. It was beyond his reach. When he sat on his knees ready to give up, it was the first time I could see how bald he was, how I could picture that hat on his head and not hair.

I hurled a rope with a life preserver I found on one of the boats along the dock and jumped in the water. I crawled through the foam ring and began to swim as fast as I could toward the hat, my arms chopping into the water, but he yanked the rope attached to it. I never felt so determined and so helpless at the same time.

"Let me go," I said, pushing aside the water in front of me, splashing myself in the face.

Nonno stood there with his hands on his head. I followed his eyes to the hat. It wasn't brown anymore. It shone like a deep green gemstone, and the water was clear enough to reflect it. Even the feather seemed to fill out like a tree that goes from winter to spring. I don't know where all the mud went, but the river was a piece of crystal now.

"I'm almost there! Let me get it for you!"

He heard me but didn't let go of the rope. I think he saw something he never expected to see in his life again. His skinny lips swooped up on both sides in the shape of a canoe, and that made me stop all my kicking and splashing. When he took his hands off his bare head and let them rest at his side, I just floated on the glassy river as still as can be. All I wanted to do was let him watch his hat drift down the river like an emerald mountain.

"Look, Nonno! Agosto's green!"

He reached up, touched his head, and pretended to tip his hat to old man Agosto. As my grandfather mimed this gesture not once or twice but three times, I imagined his green felt hat floating downstream all the way to the confluence where three rivers meet.

In the name of the Allegheny, and of the Monongahela, and of the Ohio. Amen.

Jesus behind Bars

Not far from St. Patrick's Roman Catholic Church, from its sanctuary smells of melting wax and replica of Rome's Holy Stairs where worshipers ascend on their knees, Jesus is behind bars, his nose rubbing against an iron fence on Liberty Avenue. But everyone long ago stopped trying to set him free, believing this is just one more cross for their Savior to bear. Everyone except for Aida Estella Del Negro, an old woman who spots the life-sized statue on her way back from buying two chickens at a live poultry market in Pittsburgh's Strip District.

Normally Aida Estella doesn't leave her own river town, let alone ride a bus to the city, but for Easter she must cook live chickens and prepare a feast like she's never done before. She is accustomed to making a ham with pineapple slices and candied sweet potatoes after a dish of ravioli, but this year she will cook meat as white as the Easter lily in memory of her husband Giorgio, who died last year at the age of eighty-eight, three days after the Resurrection. More than any other Easter, she wants to celebrate its miracle. She hasn't prepared live chickens in years, yet she believes that she must start with life to witness death and the wonder of rebirth.

She boards the bus whose route along the river will take her to a strip of fish and poultry markets. Once settled in her seat, she pulls out her pocket Bible and rereads the passage where Jesus rises from the dead. She thinks of him moving that boulder and breaking out of the cave and figures it might as well have been a prison with bars and barbed wire.

And she thinks of the time her husband fell into a deep crevice in the dry earth of their San Procopio and how her eldest daughter, Celestina, found him buried in its rock and rubble, how old man Agosto pulled Giorgio out as if he too rose from the dead. She closes the Bible and pictures two roasted chickens in the center of her dining room table with enough food to feed her children and grandchildren.

She stares out the window, knowing nothing about the city except that there are new immigrants here as she once was. She's heard them being called "boat people," which reminds her of how she and her family were stowed in the basement of a steamship for eighteen days. There was only enough room to stand like a candle with your arms pressed against your side. She remembers the smell of vomit and disease mixed with salt water. As miserable as that was, she is convinced that the fear of falling off a raft and drowning in the middle of the ocean like so many Cubans have done must be worse. These immigrants, she's seen on the news, make their own boats from inner tubes and scraps of canvas and wood. And why do they risk their lives? The only answer that comes to Aida Estella's mind is faith. They believed, like she believed, that when one life ends in the old country, a new one begins in America.

The hesitation her husband had leaving his San Procopio is no different from the hesitation the new immigrants had stepping into a boat. And neither, in Aida Estella's mind, is different from her husband's reluctance to let go after being in a coma for weeks.

She knows next to saying goodbye to her parents in the old country so many years ago, the hardest thing she's ever done was to release her husband. He was comatose. He gritted his teeth. His arms were stiff and his hands were in fists. She forced one open, told him it was time. His body was nothing more than a cage that trapped his spirit. It served no purpose anymore other than to hold him back. That he should be set free.

She could never muster the courage to tell him that until Easter Sunday. Three days later, he died. All of this reassures her doubts of being on a bus en route to a place she's never been with nothing more than her broken English. She must begin with live chickens and go to the only place her butcher says she will find them.

As soon as Aida Estella spots bushel baskets and crates from the bus window, she figures that she's reached the warehouse district and waves her hand at the driver. She gets off at the next stop and tightens the apron around her waist before she begins walking. Her back hunches over. Her feet turn out, but as she breathes through her mouth, she funnels enough air to keep two people alive.

Her head turns from one side of the street to the other as she searches for a live poultry market. She does this for a couple of blocks, then hears clucking ahead of her. She follows the sound a few doors down and enters.

Aida Estella walks slowly up and down the aisle and begins to sneeze from the feathers everywhere—embroidering the red tile floors, nesting in empty egg cartons, floating in the air like tattered kites. There's even a feather slowly landing on her shoulder as if it were a snowflake about to melt on concrete.

The chickens are caged on one side, the hens on the other. In between dangles a round, metal scale on which they are weighed.

Aida Estella stops to watch the birds dip their heads into a long tray with bits of kernels. She is taken by the hens and how their thin red plumes flutter. More than the clacking, she hears the rattling sound of the birds' thick claws scraping against the metal cages. She points to the two she will buy and cook up for her Easter feast: a pair with their beaks poking through the cage, searching for something other than feed.

"If you could pay now, please," the clerk says. He knows that she won't be able to reach inside her pocketbook once she has a chicken in each hand, two loose chickens that have been penned up for so long.

She opens the clasp on her change purse and hands him a roll of bills with a gum band wrapped around it. He slips the wad in his pocket, releases the hatch on the cage, and grabs her two chickens.

"I fix?" she asks.

The clerk reminds her how to clean and dress the chickens. Aida Estella may not understand all his words, but she watches every hand movement he makes. Now she remembers what to do.

"I fix," she says when he finishes the demonstration.

Aida Estella clutches the birds under her armpits as she walks toward the bus stop, taking small steps so her stride doesn't give the chickens the momentum to escape. She knows that each must be waiting for her to ease up so it can slip through the ring of her arm like a circus animal through a hoop. It doesn't take long before the chickens come to feel the strength of her grip. Another block, they tuck their feet under their bodies and settle into the warmth of her bosom. For the time being, they are stone in her hands.

Aida Estella makes her way along the Strip back to the bus stop. The walk keeps the chickens calm as they pass by candy and coffee shops, wooden crates of Chinese cabbage, pots of purple hyacinths, and smells of Italian bread and Indian spices, of sizzling kebobs and lavender from the arts and crafts boutique, the record store playing Frank Sinatra. She glances down to see that the birds have been lulled to sleep.

The next block, she allows herself to enjoy all the wares spread out on sidewalk tables—sparkling pins and earrings, books and music tapes, boxes of black and gold flags—and a man with a top hat seated in a high chair, selling square cushions the same colors.

He calls out to her, "Just look, don't buy! Just look, don't buy!"

As she walks closer, he lowers his voice when he sees that the chickens are asleep in her arms.

The next vendor is offering samples of biscotti drizzled with chocolate and filled with pistachio nuts and pieces of apricot. He sees her eyeing them but with no free hand to reach for one. The man wraps one in a napkin and slips it in her coat pocket. She thanks him and keeps walking.

The chickens nestled in her bosom make her think of all the times she carried her twins in her arms when they were babies. How they rested so peacefully when she nursed them or took them with her to the water fountain, how now their children push their children in carriages and feed them bottles filled with powder and water.

She looks straight ahead on Liberty Avenue and notices a steeple not far away. She passes the church where so many people visit. They walk through the open doors and dip their finger in holy water before walking up the aisle to the altar. Aida Estella would like to make the sign of the cross when she sees a crucifix below a stained glass window, but she bows her head and genuflects instead. God forgives. He knows these chickens that fill her arms are to celebrate life after death, for Jesus and for her Giorgio.

It is then she spots the life-sized statue of a man leaning up against an iron gate. His hands reach out through the bars as if he is begging for a handout. Steps closer, she sees he is wearing a cloak the color of eggplant and a crown of thorns. A red dot is centered on the palms of his cupped hands. He wears his heart on his robe. She stops and looks in horror into his almond-shaped eyes gazing down at the concrete sidewalk through the bars. This statue of Jesus reminds Aida Estella of her husband in a coma—the stiff arms and the palms of his hands facing up, the blank stare in his eyes.

She is so horrified that she forgets her hold on the chickens and puts her hands on her head. She screams to set him free.

"Fallu u vaji!"

The chickens hit concrete. They are stunned and still half-asleep. Aida Estella reaches down to pick them up when she hears the clucks at her feet. She sings a lullaby to try to calm them down and scoops one up in her arm, but it slips out when she reaches down to snatch the other. She tries again. This time, both birds walk away from her.

She walks after them, but as slow as they are, she is not quick enough to catch them.

The birds are waking up and begin to flap themselves to the hood of a pickup truck, their feathers floating in the air above her head. Aida Estella spots a vendor wheeling a hot dog cart with a huge gold and blue umbrella across the street. With one eye on her chickens and the other ahead, she hurries over to the woman when she spots a magnet of Christ on the cross sticking to the shiny counter. A drop of ketchup is splattered on it.

Aida Estella taps the woman on the shoulder and asks for help. "*Nu minutu pe favuri. Aiutami.*"

The woman shakes her head and keeps wheeling her cart; the stem of the umbrella wiggles back and forth despite the duct tape wrapped around it.

"*Chiama la poliziu. Nejati,*" Aida Estella says as quickly as the woman bolts across the street.

The vendor doesn't understand Italian, but she's lived in the neighborhood long enough to know what the fuss is about.

"I know. I know. What a shame," she says, picking up a bag of buns that slid off the counter. She crosses the street when the light turns green and parks herself outside an office building for the lunchtime crowd.

"*I mei pulli. My chickens!*" Aida Estella yells. She stops in the middle of the street and wipes her brow with a handkerchief, waving it as the driver of a senior citizens van stops in front of her to see if she needs a ride. She peers in the window and sees a holy card clipped on the driver's visor. A rosary is wrapped around the rearview mirror along with pink fuzzy dice.

She signals to the driver for help. He puts the van in park and steps out. He follows her, then stops because she is going in two different directions—toward Jesus behind bars and back toward her chickens now up on the roof of the truck. She grabs the driver's arm, but he shakes his head and mumbles something about her not knowing if she is coming or going. She asks him to call the police right away. To set Jesus free and to catch her chickens.

An anxious passenger beeps the horn and accidentally releases the emergency brake, so the van drifts toward the driver and Aida Estella, who still won't let go of his arm. He breaks her hold and runs after the van. Another passenger steps on the brake, and the van stops. The driver hops in and speeds away.

Three boys walk toward Aida Estella, who is now standing on the sidewalk between Jesus and her chickens. Their T-shirts are loose, their pants are baggy, and their athletic socks sag below their ankles. They take turns kicking an old battery box, a "Delco Freedom Fighter," as if it were a soccer ball. Thank God, she thinks, they are wearing holy medals around their necks next to World Cup buttons pinned on their shirts. She accidentally kicks the battery box when she asks them if they speak Italian. The box hits the parked truck, scaring the chickens into flight once again.

All they hear is the word Italian.

"Argentina is *numero uno*," one boy says.

She points to Jesus behind bars. "Free," she says.

"Say what?" he asks.

"No free," she says, pointing to her chickens.

"Make up your mind, lady."

The boys sprint after the chickens, which are now on top of a garbage heap. The three boys each take turns trying to scale the dumpster. Aida Estella watches with her hands pressed against her cheek. One boy hooks his foot at the top of the dumpster and she breaks into a cheer as he thrusts his whole body up.

"*Numero uno*," she says, thrashing her pocketbook like a pom-pom.

The boy grabs the leg of a chair on the heap to help him stand up, but tumbles backward and lands in his friends' arms below. They shrug their shoulders and run off.

Aida Estella grabs a board from the dumpster and begins poking at the chickens, but they fly to a limb of a nearby tree. She walks up to the house where Jesus is behind bars and knocks on the door. First with her knuckles, then with her fists, rapping again and again, but nobody answers. She walks over to Jesus and tries to stand him upright so his face isn't against the bars. Although the statue is hollow, it's too awkward for her to move. She waits for someone who lives in the house to come home. Or for someone to climb the tree and snatch those chickens. Every so often she shakes the tree, thinking they will fall into her arms.

Aida Estella corners the next person she sees walking down the street, a Hasidic Jew. He says he can do nothing for Jesus, but he goes to a kosher store to get a ladder to rescue her chickens. When he returns, they have elevated themselves to a rung on a telephone pole.

"That high up," he says, unfolding his ladder. He climbs the six steps up and stretches his arms only to find he is an arm's length too short.

"*I mei pulli*," Aida Estella calls out.

"We need a bigger ladder," he answers, as the chickens are now perched on a rooftop.

Aida's eyes follow the rungs of the ladder up to the top and she thinks how her husband overcame his fear of heights and climbed up to his wounded mother on the roof. The courage he had. If only she could figure out a way to get up there and bring those chickens down for him.

She runs to get a broom she spots on a porch and reaches it up to the Hasid, motioning for him to use it to poke at the chickens.

"They'll just go higher. Then you'll ask me to scale the chimney," he tells her.

Live chickens for Giorgio. She needs the live chickens. Aida reaches in her pocket for the biscotti wrapped up in a napkin. She breaks it in half and reaches up to hand it to the man.

"*I mei pulli*," she says again.

"Wouldn't it be easier to just buy two more at the poultry market?" he asks.

Once the man's feet touch the earth, she helps tuck in his shirt before walking over to the statue of Jesus behind bars.

"That's where your chickens should be," he says, folding up the ladder to return to the kosher store.

Aida Estella takes her wallet out of her pocketbook to see if she has enough money to buy two more chickens. She doesn't.

She takes out a tissue from her purse and wipes the dust inside the statue's cupped palms. She tries again to stand Jesus up so his face isn't leaning against the bars. This time she positions herself at a different angle and pushes it upright. The statue's eyes look into hers, and hers look up to feast on the sight of her two chickens, a bounty of golden wings rising up into the arms of the sun.

Catina's Haircut

There once was an Italian woman named Catina who had most unusual hair. From the front, she looked like any other woman her age. She had black-framed glasses, a shade of rouge to give her cheeks some color, and a flowered silk scarf over her head, her soft, gray curls slipping out to drape her face. She wore a tweed jacket, a pair of stretch slacks, and comfortable shoes for running errands on Liberty Avenue. Catina wheeled a buggy and was often seen with stacks of neatly folded laundry or groceries she bought at the specialty shops in Bloomfield—homemade ricotta cheese, hot sausage links, bottles of hazelnut syrup, and squares of tiramisu from the sweet shop. In fact, when she pushed her buggy striped in bold red, white, and green, she blended right in with the fire hydrants, curbs, and light posts painted the same colors in Pittsburgh's Little Italy.

But from the back, one couldn't help but notice her hair. Below her three-corner scarf was a thick tail of it that fell below her knees. At the bottom was a mound of braids tied with a red ribbon so her hair wouldn't drag on the ground when she walked. Some say her hair was the color of a mudslide during the rainy season and others who touched it said it was as hard as the rocky soil of a Calabrian hill town in a drought.

When she was a young woman of twenty, Catina had stopped cutting her hair. Fifty years ago, to date. They say it grew so long because her great-grandmother Annunziata, who was a sorceress in San Procopio, had brewed a tonic of roots strong enough to pass on to the generation that would one day come to America. And if Catina drank it while standing in a riverbed, in water high enough to cover her knees, her hair would grow all the years the crops in her hill town hadn't from lack of rain.

And the day she stopped cutting her hair was the day she stopped combing it, because there wasn't a brush big enough for her to use.

The story goes that as a child Catina had the thickest and fastest-growing hair from drinking her great-grandmother's tonic. It shone so brightly, like a shaft of wheat in the sun, that you could see your reflection in one strand of Catina's hair more clearly than in a full-length mirror.

During the day, it grew so fast that hats popped off her head. Everyone in the neighborhood gave her the nickname Capilli. And her hair was so thick that even the red ribbon passed on from her great-grandmother was barely strong enough to keep it bundled into a ponytail. Her hair blanketed every inch of her pillow when she went to bed at night.

When she was a child, her mother took her to the barber for a haircut every other week. Like many immigrant families struggling in the new country, Catina's mother sold her hair to people placing ads in the paper who could afford wigmakers to weave them custom-made ringlets and curls.

Catina begged her mother to let her hair grow, because in those days, the girls with short, cropped "bowl cuts" were taken for the poor immigrants that they were. Chopping off a child's hair to sell it suited not only the immigrant family pocketbook but also government officials who inspected children for lice and other pests festering in the wooden row houses.

In those days, hair length was a measure of social position. The longer, the wealthier the girl, for she had maids who spent hours washing, rinsing, combing, and fussing over her locks, tying them with silk and velvet bows that matched her feathered hats. Catina resented these girls and their bouquets of curls because they held their heads up so high, as if they'd rather stare into space than look into someone's eyes.

Catina also resented her family for coming to Pittsburgh. She didn't care that they lived in a plateau high above the Allegheny River named after all the wild flowers that used to bloom there. All she saw were run-down row houses built for the mill workers on narrow streets.

"If we would have stayed in San Procopio, we wouldn't be so poor," she told her mother.

"We would be poorer. When farmers in Calabria reach out their hands for something in return for their labor, they're filled with calluses and not food," her mother said.

Every time Catina was to go to the barbershop to get her head shaved, she hid from her mother. She snuck behind the French doors and the potbelly stove, in the broom closet and the fruit cellar, inside the trunk, and in sacks of semolina flour. Each time, Catina found a new place to hide, and each time, her mother found her, cuffed her wrist with her hand, and yanked her to the barber. Catina swore that as soon as she could "lie her age" and find work, she'd leave home.

When she was fifteen, Catina quit school and began working for a landlord, cleaning and waxing three flights of stairs in the apartment building where she lived. On her knees, she started at the bottom and worked her way up. Her pay was the basement room the landlord gave her. So for five more years, Catina continued to go to the barber and sell her hair, using the money to buy food. She was too ashamed to admit this to her mother, so Catina never once visited home.

At the time, she had met Leonard Wexler. Leonard's father worked for the Sears-Roebuck Catalog Company selling blueprints for two-story houses and bungalows. Leonard promised to marry Catina when she grew her hair to her shoulders, just like the pictures of women in his father's catalogs. Catina knew that even her hair would take months to grow, and she had no way to feed herself for that long if she didn't sell it. She knew she had abandoned her family and couldn't go back to live with them. And the day Catina got a good-paying job at the mill was the day her fiancé got drafted.

She grew her hair, hoping that he'd return from the war and marry her like he had promised. She wrote him letters each week, reporting on how many inches it had to grow until it reached her shoulders. He never answered, and when the war ended, she took the bus to the city to meet the returning soldiers, her hair bouncing off her shoulders. There she learned from Leonard's commanding officer that he was killed in battle.

At the age of seventy, Catina walked with her head up high but not due to her social position, as she worked the same mill for nearly fifty years. It was because her hair was so heavy that she strained her neck to hold up its weight. She began to wear a brace, but eventually, even it didn't keep her head from tilting back. She no longer could see the ground she stood on, her neighbors or their houses. She looked into the empty sky and made her way by finding the church steeple at St. Joseph's or the Bloomfield Bridge, high enough for her to see. It was as though she walked around in blindness and needed a cane to guide her through the streets.

Only when her mother died did Catina lose her desire to grow her hair any longer. She came to realize how it kept her from being a loving daughter, a member of her community, and a wife. Any man attracted to Catina had been quickly scared away by the weapon her hair could be. One swing and she could strike him down as if he were a bowling pin.

She decided it was time to cut it, that if nothing else in life, maybe this would make her happy. She walked briskly and headed straight for the glare of the red, white, and blue glass pole spinning outside of Dan Cercone's barbershop. She knocked on the door and was let in.

"What can I do for you today?" asked the barber, his eyes plunging to the ground to meet the end of Catina's hair.

"The last time a barber cut my hair, he cut it all off," she told the barber.

"That had to be many, many years ago," he said.

"Fifty, to be exact."

"And you want me to cut it?" he asked.

She struggled to nod her head.

"You tell me how much and I'll cut," he promised.

The barber helped Catina take a seat. He felt the weight of her hair when he lifted it to wrap a smock around her shoulders.

"Your hair must tip the scales," the barber commented.

"Some people are worth their weight in gold or in love. I have nothing but my hair," Catina said.

The barber pumped the chair up with his foot hundreds of times, until Catina was practically touching the ceiling. Her hair still brushed the floor. The brought out the sharpest pair of scissors he could find in his drawer.

"Cut two feet off," she said, her voice echoing off the ceiling.

He opened the scissors wide and squeezed the handle with all his might. The shears snapped in two. He reached into the drawer and tried another pair.

"Make that three feet," Catina said.

Again, he opened the scissors wide and squeezed the handle, this time using both hands. The shears snapped. He reached into the drawer and tried yet another pair. But first, he sharpened them until the blade could split the air in two.

"Make that four feet," Catina said. Each time the barber ruined a pair of shears, Catina added another foot for him to cut off. She was up to eight feet when the barber said he had run out of scissors and his wrists had become sore from the pressure.

"I thought you were the best-known barber in Little Italy," she yelled down to him.

"That is what they tell me."

"And hairstylist of the year," she added.

"Yes, but you need to go to a specialist with the right kind of . . . tools," the barber said.

"Like who?" Catina asked, her eyelashes brushing the ceiling.

"Someone who prunes trees and bushes might be able to help you," he said.

"What barber does that?"

He suggested she try a groundskeeper at Allegheny Cemetery.

"A groundskeeper!"

The barber brought Catina down and removed the plastic smock. Cross-eyed from staring so close to the ceiling, she fumbled in her pocketbook for her wallet to pay him for six pairs of broken scissors. He guided her to the door and pointed her in the right direction.

Catina stumbled up and down every street in the neighborhood, looking for another barber to cut her hair. But by the time she managed to find one, he had already heard about the one at Dan Cercone's who broke all his shears and sprained his wrists trying.

Desperate, she bought all kinds of tools she could find in the hardware store and tried them all—hacksaws, chisels, hedge clippers. They wilted when they touched her hair.

She had one tool left: a scythe like the one her father used day after day to cut wheat and brush in the slopes of Calabria. It was only when she used that tool on her hair that she came to realize the reason her father brought his family to this country. She cut until blisters formed between every one of her fingers. Her arms grew so tired and numb she couldn't move them. Exhausted, she went to bed without a single hair cut.

The following day, Catina woke up, remembering how the barber had told her to go to someone who prunes trees and bushes, a groundskeeper at Allegheny Cemetery. She thought it was ridiculous when he told her then, but now she was desperate for help.

With her head still tilted toward the sky, Catina made her way to the cemetery's entrance by following the sound of the bells ringing in its Courthouse tower. She continued through the gate and stayed on the pavement but knew she'd have to veer off into the greenery to find a gardener. She stumbled through rows and rows of gravestones made of bronze and granite and marble. Each time she nicked one, she visualized the tip of her shoe touching letters that spelled the names of Civil War soldiers, Pittsburgh mayors, all the famous people buried there. Catina tried to bow her head out of respect for the dead. The weight of her hair made this impossible, as she was weary and could not muster the strength. She made the sign of the cross and moved on.

Catina listened for the snap of tree branches or the rustling of a bush, but there was silence. She must have been walking by mausoleums and obelisks, monuments and statues. She kept walking until she heard the sound of digging. She walked in that direction and asked the landscaper for his help.

He didn't say a word, but she could hear him put his shovel to rest.

"You'll need that," she said, and repeated her request.

The man could not speak English, but he understood what she wanted as soon as she turned around and he saw hair all the way down her legs.

"Please cut it for me," she asked the man.

Catina lay on the ground while the man cut through the twists of her hair with his shovel as if he were breaking rocky soil. She stood up with shoulder-length hair, looked this immigrant worker in the eyes, and thanked him for doing what nobody else had the strength to do.

When he smiled, she got on her knees and reached down, not to touch her hair but the earth in his shovel.

Flash Light

From the kitchen window, Maria Ungaro spots someone
dart past the lilac bush toward her back door and is so startled
that she drops a spoon into a pitcher of juice. Citrus drops splash
Maria Ungaro in the eye as her neighbor pounds on the door with
the meaty side of her fist. She opens it, squinting.

Maria Ungaro can make out Audrey by her stretch pants with
permanent creases and the pastel colors she wears that remind her of
those fruit-flavored miniature marshmallows women in the neighborhood use in their five-cup salads. A scarf tied at the back of
Audrey's neck pulls the hair away from her face, except for identical
spit-curl sideburns resting on her cheeks. Her white canvas Keds
smell from a fresh coat of nurse's shoe polish.

Maria Ungaro dabs her eyes with a washcloth and asks her neighbor if she'll join her and her husband, Leoluca, for breakfast. A plate
of cantaloupe and honeydew slices is at the center of the table.

"I've eaten, thank you," says Audrey, staring down at the stained
cloth Maria Ungaro bunches up in her hand.

"Coffee?"

"No caffeine for me," Audrey answers.

"Please. Have a seat," Maria Ungaro insists, sliding out a chair. Leoluca, wearing a napkin tucked in his navy blue work shirt and dunking a bread crust in a bowl of coffee, is silent after a perfunctory greeting.

"I thought you should know. You have wasps," Audrey says, still standing in the doorway.

Maria Ungaro's voice drops. "Is that why you're here?"

"That . . . and to say hello. Look, I didn't mean to interrupt breakfast. Take a look when you're finished," she says, about to leave.

"Let's see." Maria Ungaro rushes to her kitchen window. Her eyes pan across her porch before she zeroes in on the insects, circling above the welcome mat she had washed and set out to dry.

"They multiply if you don't kill them first," Audrey says, choking the neck of the doorknob with her hand.

Maria Ungaro lifts a tray of struffoli from the counter and passes the mound of honey balls over to her neighbor.

"Thanks, but I wouldn't know how to begin to eat those."

"Are you sure I can't offer you something, Audrey? It's been so long since we've talked. How are your boys? Are they doing well?"

"Oh my, yes. They're good kids."

Audrey doesn't ask about Maria Ungaro's own two sons, too far away to visit home other than on holidays. Her eldest is in Springfield, Ohio, in roofing, and her youngest in Angola, New York, in TV repair. Maria Ungaro places her index finger on her top lip. "My sons are both out of state. This country is too big. Too much room to fly away."

Audrey sees herself out. "It isn't big enough," she mutters, bolting past the wasps still hovering around the welcome mat.

As soon as Audrey is out of sight, Leoluca says his first complete sentence of the day: "You're going to have to spray."

Maria Ungaro turns around to face him. He gulps, his eyes hidden behind his bowl of coffee, and points with his chin to the window overlooking the wasps.

"They're just passing by," she says.

"They're building a nest. You have to spray before they get too comfortable."

Maria Ungaro's black waves of hair fringe her heart-shaped face. As she gazes out the window at the wasps, her eyebrows rise in wonder.

"Just because you build a new home doesn't mean you get comfortable, Leo."

She turns to face her husband. He is a man who no matter the time of day is never without his five o'clock shadow. When Leoluca was old enough, he left Italy and found work in the steel mill and sent for Maria Ungaro five and a half years later. By that time, he was friends with all the guys in his union. They went deer hunting and trout fishing and beer gardening together. In fact, there were more deer heads and fishing plaques hanging on the walls in the Ungaro house than pictures of the couple and their sons.

Leoluca sent Maria Ungaro postcards of the Statue of Liberty when he first arrived in this country, but she had no idea this area was so different from New York City or even Pittsburgh proper, where she had hoped they would live. Maybe Little Italy in the neighborhood of Bloomfield. There or closer to her cousins, Celestina and her brother and sisters who settled in Tarentum, a Pittsburgh area river town up the Allegheny years before she came to this country.

At least in the city, she imagined there were so many people that she'd never feel alone. Not on the sidewalks, on the bus, in the markets, or apartment buildings. Not even on a park bench. But in this area, there was so much land between houses. Especially in suburban hills where Leoluca bought one without telling her while she was still in Italy.

Late for work, Leoluca raises his cup in a mock toast to his wife. He leaves her with her back framed in the window, staring at the wasps. She's mesmerized, closely observing the insects in the sun's glare during the day and in a beaming flashlight in the dark. Their slender, honey-colored bodies are marked with thick, steel blue bands. Wings unfold and move like fans gently waving on a breeze. Their faces are long, their legs wiry. Their bulging eyes never blink, never dim, never look away. Always connected to hers.

The nest the worker wasps assemble outside Maria Ungaro's kitchen window is pear-shaped with interior combs, rows of cells several stories high, lined up as evenly as windows in an apartment building. She watches as they chew tree bark and the fibers of plants until their saliva dissolves them to a pulp to build a nest, layer upon layer of ridges. Gray on top of brown on top of white on top of shale, the consistency of felt and yet massive enough for a queen and nearly four hundred wasps. Maria Ungaro counts them.

The wasps crawl inside their nest at 4:30 every afternoon to cool off, their translucent wings vanishing in the dark. At 6:30 they reappear at their cell windows to continue looping threads and slivers of tree bark.

The way in which these insects move when they work convinces Maria Ungaro that they communicate with one another. She spots the eggs through the holes of the nest—one laid in every cell—and is fascinated at how the queen carefully cleans them from the top down, licking off the liquid. Once the eggs hatch, the queen chews up pieces of insects and brings them to the larvae for food. Maria Ungaro marvels at how the larvae spin cocoons around themselves before they emerge as full-grown wasps. It all reminds her of her dreams of the lively piazza of her childhood in Sinopoli.

In the setting sun, colors fade. Neighbors are cast in a golden glow. Shadows inked on stone, their legs and arms are so elongated that no matter their true shape or size, they are the same distorted black figures. Slowly, their shadows come to life. Everyone takes a few steps forward and then stops to talk with their neighbors before advancing a few more steps only to pause for another visit. Steps repeated enough times for a rhythm to develop, a choreographed dance everyone follows in one another's eyes. The shadows swirl around their golden bodies, spinning themselves in circles. The whirring of dresses and pant legs becomes a melodious hum that is louder than words. And just as they knew when to begin, everyone simultaneously stops when the dance has ended.

No. Maria Ungaro won't destroy the nest the wasps built on the glass of her kitchen window, even if it means being at odds with her neighbor. She would only be fooling herself if she thought there was a friendship in jeopardy. Before Audrey's visit about the wasps, the last time she had stepped inside Maria Ungaro's home or vice versa was nearly ten years ago when the Ungaros offered to build a big gazebo for their neighbors. Maria Ungaro wanted it to be a place for them to picnic together and listen to music and dance on weekends. She was so elated at the thought of bringing her neighbors together that she volunteered to buy the picnic tables and sew cushions.

"You can't build a piazza, Maria," Leoluca warned her. "You're not in Italy no more. These people don't go for that here. They keep to themselves."

To appease his wife, Leoluca offered to build the gazebo if she managed to talk her neighbors into it. The way he figured, they would never consent to giving up even the smallest corner of their backyard if that meant losing their privacy. And if by some miracle they did agree, it would buy him more freedom when his wife had a social circle of her own like the one she left behind in Sinopoli.

In Sinopoli, Maria Ungaro and her neighbor and best friend, Silvia, had daily conversations out of their third-floor windows as they watered the geraniums in the flowerboxes. When one opened the shutters, it was like picking up the phone. They talked for more than an hour, holding sprinkling cans instead of receivers. They held three-way conversations with people passing by on the cobbled street below. Sometimes, the two would take turns tossing dreams far enough to land on the golden fringes of sunflowers in the fields nearby.

Other days, they embroidered pillowcases or Maria Ungaro would show Silvia her latest sewing project by wheeling a wicker basket over to her, using a pulley system. Silvia lifted a white veil and beaded headdress from the basket; that's how she first learned of Maria Ungaro's parents' plans for her to marry. How Silvia cried.

Maria Ungaro wondered how her new house in America would look, if it would be similar to the one in Sinopoli—the wall tiles her father hand painted, the exposed beams on the ceilings with notches carved during birthday celebrations, one for every year of every member of the family. There were the windows that faced the piazza and the ones in the back of their house above the ditch all the neighbors had helped dig for their families to take cover when American planes dropped bombs during World War II. She couldn't forget the dank smell of dirt and crying much of the night until her father pleaded with her to stop because he said her tears would flood their hole and bring them closer to the surface.

When Maria Ungaro was a child, all the neighboring adults had visited her house, since her family was one of the few in Sinopoli with a radio. All the children came there too, because school was held in their living room.

These memories were the reason Maria Ungaro came up with the idea of a community gazebo when she first came to America. In her sleep, she frequently dreamed about building one. Long, narrow boards faced every direction. Thousands of nails were splattered, and tools had no handles. The yard was a jagged surface of color from permanent green to the dullness of wood to a reflective sheen of metal. What she found most astounding was that nothing was touching, not even the strands of hair of all the neighbors somehow buried underneath the materials and tools for the gazebo. All was still until suddenly everyone emerged, simultaneously lifting walls that rose toward the sky.

Once Maria Ungaro learned to speak English, she made a list of neighbors to visit. Equipped with fabric samples, sketches, photographs of her Sinopoli piazza, and furniture catalogs, she paid her first visit to her next-door neighbor Audrey. She was counting on this being a soft sell given the fact they both had boys about the same age. However, it hadn't occurred to her that Audrey might be appalled that the underage Ungaro boys were allowed to drink wine at their supper table and to go to disco clubs on Saturday nights. What Maria Ungaro couldn't get through to Audrey was that the Sons of Italy was nothing like a disco.

Maria Ungaro gently tapped Audrey's storm door a dozen times before her neighbor answered, cracking it open a few inches and holding it there with the tip of her pointy shoe. It was clear that Maria Ungaro would not be invited in, so she spoke through the narrow opening, slipping her gazebo samples and diagrams through sideways.

"We're building a deck this summer as a matter of fact. A place for the boys to play where I can watch them," Audrey said.

"We build together," Maria Ungaro said. "For all."

"Please. I'm not interested in having a boardwalk in my backyard and neither is anyone else in this neighborhood. We want to keep the trouble out, you see, not invite it in."

"It is a place to sit and talk. Dance. Play the cards."

Audrey added that a permit was necessary and the planning board would never grant permission for such a project.

Maria Ungaro was so discouraged that she retreated to her sewing room, where she spent most of her time keeping busy at the machine with fabric art projects. She seldom saw her neighbors, because they didn't shop at the farmers' market or go to the Catholic Mass on Sunday.

Now, a second visit from Audrey doesn't surprise Maria Ungaro like the first one did.

"I'm sorry, but that nest has got to go. It's dangerous," Audrey insists.

"Wasps are not dangerous, Audrey. Not unless you frighten them."

"I don't want them in my yard!"

"Have you ever seen a wasp's nest up close?" Maria Ungaro asks.

"I can't say that I have. And I want it to stay that way."

"I even saw the queen wasp looking for the perfect place for her nest. She chose my kitchen window."

"It had to land somewhere and that somewhere happened to be here," Audrey says.

Maria Ungaro shakes her head over and over again ever so slightly, for she believes this was not random.

"I don't want to argue with you about how they got here, Maria. What matters is you see to it that they're gone. Either you destroy that nest, or I'll have to report you to the health department."

Picking up a can of spray, but only for cleaning her window, Maria Ungaro wipes all the smudges from propping her forehead against it to watch the wasps. When she steps outside onto the porch, they fly in droves, circling a crown above her head, but Maria Ungaro isn't afraid. And they aren't afraid of her. They follow her, form a procession, a long buzzing veil, black beaded with wings of silk. She walks down the path of patio stones slowly, as if stepping down a church aisle on her wedding day.

Maria Ungaro and her husband argue after they get a letter in the mail from the health department.

"They're not hurting anyone, Leo."

"I'm not paying no fine. It's settled. You hear me? If you don't get rid of that nest, I'll do it for you," he tells her.

He won't get near them, Maria Ungaro thinks to herself. He never stays in the house long enough to do anything. He won't follow through with this household chore like he hasn't with planting the rose bushes or painting the birdbath.

She hangs a sheet on the clothesline to cover the nest while she thinks of ways to avoid the health department. But this only invites Audrey's attention.

"Can I offer you something to drink?" Maria Ungaro asks as soon as Audrey is within speaking distance.

"What's behind that sheet?"

"I'm hanging clothes."

"Don't tell me you didn't get rid of that nest," Audrey says, trying to peek through.

Before Maria Ungaro can stop her, Audrey yanks the sheet from the line with the sweeping motion of a magician pulling a tablecloth out from under a set of china. The clothespins shoot into the air, and one hits the nest. The wasps disperse across the sky like a heavy black snowfall. Audrey hides behind the corner, holding her hands over her head until the wasps fall into line behind Maria Ungaro.

"I told you, they aren't dangerous," she says as her neighbor screams in disbelief all the way back to her house.

It isn't long before a man ensconced in a one-piece suit, bee-keeper's mask, gloves, and tank of spray strapped to his back knocks on Maria Ungaro's door. She pleads with the health department official to fine her the maximum amount if she can relocate the nest away from her neighbor.

"You were issued a warning. Step back, please," he says as he raises the nozzle and aims at the nest.

"They aren't hurting anyone! They'll be gone by the end of summer."

The man lifts his heavily padded arm and aims with his spray gun. "I'd suggest you go inside and close all your windows and doors. This will take a minute. And then it will be over," he assures her.

Maria Ungaro goes into the house. She only comes back out after she hears the health official tossing the nest in the garbage. She retrieves the gray flaky mass from the bin.

"I wouldn't touch that if I were you," he warns.

The concrete is covered with a mosaic of dead wasps. Maria Ungaro runs through the grass to a few she hears buzzing on the ground and moves them to a jar with honey. A day later, they die.

She places the nest in a shoebox in her sewing room, where she stares at it for days. Once she closes the lid, Maria Ungaro begins re-creating it, using a needlepoint stitch of her own she calls *punto* pittore. Beginning with a flat surface and two hundred skeins of thread, she embroiders until it becomes a six-pound, lopsided, gray shape. It is as though she is doing the work of four hundred wasps.

When she finishes, Maria Ungaro takes it to the local arts center where some of her other embroidery work is exhibited, and two weeks later, she has a buyer offering six hundred dollars for the sculpture. The gallery attendant tells her that the man had looked down on her wasp nest sculpture resting on a floor platform and was so taken by it that he spent hours peering over it. He said that he couldn't wait for it to be removed from its installation, that after all those hours, all that time he was still and silent and observant, he needed to touch it.

"I don't believe it. Six hundred bucks!" Leo says.

"I can't sell it," Maria Ungaro tells her husband.

"Who's going to make an offer like that again?"

Maria Ungaro wordlessly goes back to her sewing room. She spends every evening there, with needle and thread, adding new layers to the outside like she saw the worker wasps making their nest larger for the young.

One night when the sky turns black as if fixing to storm, her lights go on the blink.

Leo calls out from the living room, "Hey, the TV's off!"

She stands up to look out the window and sees a shadow rising above their yard, then thin mirrors of lightning flashing in the darkened sky. She calls for Leo and runs outside to the porch, needle and thread in hand.

"What the hell happened?" he says. "It's not supposed to rain."

Leo doesn't really want to know, but if he did, Maria Ungaro would tell him it's not going to rain. What's above will not destroy her home with bombs or poison. This flash of light is different. It's a glimpse of what goes on in their house, in their neighborhood, who does what and for whom, just how they relate or the habits in their lives they develop in place of love.

"Whatever it is, it's blinding my eyes," Leo says, cupping his hand on his forehead in the shape of a visor before going back into the house.

Audrey runs out a few yards beyond her porch and then scurries back inside to call the police and take shelter, pulling down every blind in her house.

Maria Ungaro wraps her arms around herself as she walks to the backyard, dodging the holes Leo dug for rose bushes but hasn't taken the time to plant. She looks up, her neck bare and pale against the night, her eyes fixed on shimmers of light that blind the darkness, and she waits.

Mirage

It took exactly twenty-six minutes for a mother, a daughter, and a chicken to board a bus to San Procopio. The driver, a slight man with narrow sideburns who was sitting on a bench near the parked bus, appeared to move at a pace that habit had timed for him rather than a schedule. He pulled up his pants, tightened his long belt a notch, and opened the door for me by bumping it with his hip.

I handed him money for the ticket, which he accepted graciously as if it were a tip rather than the fare. He bunched it in his shirt pocket with his cigarettes and pointed to all the vacant seats before walking toward the *tabacchinu*. I quickly asked if the bus would leave on time and if its route would go by the *passegiata* along the water in Reggio di Calabria. He stared at my money belt before signaling me to board, no doubt thinking I was another tourist hoping to see the Fata Morgana along the Strait of Messina, which meant he knew that I knew that unless he got the bus moving, we'd probably get there too late to witness a fantastic city rising from the sea.

It was a foggy and humid morning, and the odds were as good as they were going to get for the Sicilian town of Messina across the strait to be reflected in the water and air, creating the mirage's rare occurrence. The weather in the afternoon, however, was forecasted to turn sunny, as was the remainder of my stay. I made sure the driver saw me tapping on my watch before stepping up into the bus.

After a few minutes passed and there was still no driver, I waved at him out of my window. He nodded and smiled at me from the *tabacchinu* doorway as he ducked inside the beaded curtain. I sat back down, looked at my watch, and worried that my one chance to catch a meteorological freak of nature was ticking away.

I gave him thirty more seconds and then I would get off the bus to fetch him. I'd offer to buy him a gelato and he could lick it while he drove. He'd probably use one hand to steer anyway. Even to navigate the hairpin turns along the steep cliffside to the water. Just as I was about to hop off the bus, he poked his head outside the curtain of beads at the doorway and shouted, *"Nu minutu, pe favuri, Signura."*

The driver and I obviously had the same difference of opinion over the likelihood of the Fata Morgana that my mother and father had. I remember as a little girl asking them about it. He pulled out the encyclopedia and read what he called scientific fact: "A Fata Morgana mirage is when a layer of hot air traps rays of light coming from distant objects such as rocks, which appear to be towers of a fairy-tale castle. The light rays bend as they pass from the cool, heavy air near the surface to the warm, light air above it."

He slammed the book shut and said that if the Fata Morgana were to occur, which it wouldn't, it was no miracle that it would be in Calabria. "It's full of hot air. Not just the sirocco current from Africa but from all the people down there who have nothing better to do than listen to themselves talk! And there's enough rock in the boot of Italy for a million optical illusions! Ask the *campagnolu* who work the land. Your father was one of them. I don't want to hear no more, Celestina, about castles in the sky."

When he walked off, my mother opened the encyclopedia to the page my father read from, his sweaty thumbprint still visible on the corner of the page. She inserted a small piece of onionskin paper with a few sentences handwritten so lightly the Italian words were barely visible. When I asked my mother to read it to me, she said it was the testimony of a priest who, hundreds of years ago, witnessed the Fata Morgana miracle over the Strait of Messina. "The sea, washing up the coast of Sicily, rose up like a dark mountain range. In front of the mountain, a series of white-gray pilasters appeared. Then they shrank to half their height and built arches like those of Roman aqueducts. Castles appeared above the arches, each with towers and windows before it all vanished."

She tucked the thin piece of paper into the encyclopedia as if it were a holy card marking a page in the Bible. I often heard her reciting it out loud in a cadence of prayer. Her eyes slowly closing, her lips moving ever so slightly, whispering the words so only she could hear them. One day, thinking it was visible from the river, I asked her if she would take me to the Point in Pittsburgh.

"Never, Celeste," she insisted—not only because the meteorological conditions weren't right, but nowhere in America would ever take the place of her father's Calabria.

My father was just the opposite. America was where he came to make a life for himself, and Pittsburgh could do no wrong—never mind that he was laid off two years short of collecting a full pension when the steel mills started closing down. Or the bill collectors, the bankruptcies, the loss of a way of life for a class of people. He'd rather be in his river town than anywhere in Italy. When I'd remind him of the facts, he'd tell me to just go to the river and catch hold of the current. That's a miracle that happens every day.

My father thought I was wasting my money by going to San Procopio in search of the Fata Morgana, but before my mother died, she asked me to do one last thing for her, and that was to come here and look for it. Just look for it. It was as though she didn't care if I saw it or not, but that I believed in its possibility. Like her grandmother, a revolutionary sympathizer, had believed. My mother's namesake and mine.

How could I not go and look for it when what I loved most about my mother was how she kept her faith in something despite the improbability? Not just in miracles like the Fata Morgana but in me. My life didn't have to be set in stone. She wanted me to reach my hands out, to somehow touch what was out of my grasp, to imagine that it takes hold of me. And when it rises, let it lift me up, not allow doubt to pull me down.

I got off the bus and walked toward the smoke shop, then got back on when the driver emerged with an elderly woman who had to be twice his weight. She held on to the excess strip of his buckled belt as if it were a leash. Despite walking with a stiff knee, she appeared to be leading him and not vice versa. When they got to the bus, he offered to help her up. She took one step forward, and he took two steps back to get more leverage to give her a boost. I offered to help, but he assured me in between labored breaths, "Please. No problem."

They finally made it to the first row, but the woman pitched her purse into the seat behind it. The driver held on to her with one hand and removed the front seat cushion with his free hand, kicking it to the side. I couldn't imagine why until she sat down and he propped her stiff leg through the metal frame in front of her so she could rest it on springs.

"*Tuttu o postu?*" he asked her.

She smiled.

"*Miraculu,*" he said, winking at me as if to say getting her in her seat was more of a spectacle than what I'd see at the Strait of Messina.

The elderly woman moved in her seat to reach for her pocket-book. She handed the man a sweet, then muttered something about waiting for her daughter, although her voice was lost in the swishing sound from all the air trapped inside her seat. He asked if she would need help too. She shook her head and insisted he sit down.

"*Presto. Presto,*" I pleaded.

He opened his leather pouch and recorded a couple of Roman numerals with a felt-tip pen, making each one slowly and deliberately in calligraphy as if the log were going to be hung on a museum wall. I was ready to ask him if he wanted to borrow the pastel chalks

I had in my backpack for drawing but was afraid he'd take me up on it. Already he had to fudge numbers on his schedule, because we were running late and the daughter still hadn't boarded the bus. Minutes later, she arrived, wearing a print skirt that matched her mother's top.

"*Pozzu?*" she asked the driver.

With a live chicken pressed onto her pregnant belly, she got as far as the first step when the driver pointed to the chicken and said, "*Non tu permettu.*"

The bird's yellow eyes began to water. Its feathers ruffled with anticipation. Its tail twitched with unease. Meanwhile, the mother lifted her propped leg out of the seat in front of her and dropped it to the ground. She stood up, hobbled over to the driver's seat, and plopped herself down. The three of them began clucking louder than the chicken.

I took my watch off and put it in my backpack because I didn't want to know how late we were anymore. I couldn't believe what I saw. The driver was standing on the bus step, the mother above him, the daughter below. He was in purgatory. He asked the woman to leave the chicken outside and reached for the rope to pull the door shut.

"*Spetta,*" the mother said. She grabbed on to the rearview mirror and pulled herself up from the driver's seat. She asked her daughter for the chicken. The daughter handed it to the bus driver, who held the bird for a few seconds before insisting that the daughter take the chicken back and leave it behind, or she could not get on the bus.

I offered to take the chicken and put it in my backpack so we could go. I emptied my things out of the sack and handed it to the driver.

"*Non c'e' bisognu,*" he said, asking me to please sit back down.

The mother asked the bus driver to hand her the chicken. She would take care of it. He hesitated, but before he could give it back to the daughter, the mother snatched the chicken out of his hands, wrapped her chunky fingers around the bird's neck, and snapped it like a wishbone.

"*E'cca'*," she pronounced as she signaled for the driver to sit in his seat and let her daughter on the bus. She made her way back to her seat. The mother handed me the dead chicken to hold while she sat herself down and propped her leg up. I handed it back to her, and she placed it on her daughter's lap as soon as she sat down.

Satisfied a live animal had not been brought on board, the driver started the bus, letting it drift several yards before he stepped on the gas.

I couldn't help but think of how my grandmother took a Port Authority Transit bus to the Strip District in Pittsburgh so she could buy some live chickens for an Easter meal to remember my grandfather's passing. The chickens got loose, so she didn't have to try to board the bus home with them. I can only imagine what the PAT driver would have said. Aida was a determined woman, but those chickens could have had black and gold feathers and been waving a Steelers Terrible Towel and they still wouldn't have been allowed on board.

The bus ride to San Procopio was scenic, but it was hard to settle into sightseeing on a windy, pockmarked road. The floor vibrated, and I frequently popped out of my seat. The women, on the other hand, didn't budge. Even the vineyards on the cliff we drove by somehow defied gravity by rooting themselves in the severe angle of the slope. I couldn't imagine harvesting the grapes there. One false move and it was a long tumble to the sea.

I began to wonder if I was ready to see the house in San Procopio where my mother, my uncle, and my aunts were born, where my grandfather was born, where my great-grandparents were killed during a call for revolution. Was I ready to bear witness to my family's history so that I could someday tell my children like my mother and grandfather have told me?

I couldn't deny I had this notion that San Procopio would be unawakened from its dormancy. That while the rest of the world tossed and turned with restless modernity, this hill town would sleep. It would feel quiet and lifeless. It was as if Mamà's spirit were pulling away from me the closer I got.

I began to second-guess myself. Why had I never visited San

Procopio with her when she was alive? What if I don't see this miracle she spoke of and no longer believe in its possibility? What if I fail to imagine the land my great-grandmother had the courage to envision until her death? What if I only see the dry, dusty ground under my feet?

My mother, Celestina. My great-grandmother, Celina, and their heaven. And despite their name passed on to me, would I be bound by the earth?

The bus continued on the road along the cliff, following the fishy smell of the sea to the promenade. Even from a distance, I could tell the water was so clear that I imagined dropping a penny and being able to watch it land on the bottom. There were sandy beaches, gritty cement buildings, and eroding castle fortresses. It seemed one wave could wash the city away as though it never existed. I supposed that's what the 1783 and 1908 earthquakes really did. Only the debris wasn't cleared. Instead, it mounted, and the city was laid to rest, married to the stone that buried it.

Because natural disasters leveled everything, I hadn't expected Reggio to have Old World charm or even a flavor of each of the rulers who conquered this region, a succession of foreign invasions and feudal order. Greeks. Romans. Normans. French. Spaniards. Arabs. Perhaps I'd see a ruin here or there. Some small fragment but never the whole.

No ivory cupolas rose above the fortress the way my mother said they did in San Procopio. The skyline was so uniform, not one building could reach upwards from the massive concrete heap weighted down with the rubble of history. The buildings were not what I'd call architecture but rather pale gray shells filled out of necessity. Yet my mother believed this land had something that no earthquake could crumble, no drought could evaporate, and no famine could starve: the hope of seeing the Fata Morgana.

The bus drove slowly along the promenade, and I began to look out the window for believers like my mother. Surely they too could feel the cool air near their feet clashing with the warmer air against their faces. I had this idea that there would be rows of occupied benches, all facing the sea. No newspapers. No chatting with friends. No food in their laps. They'd just sit there for hours, watching the sky as if it were an altar.

Instead, it was still quiet from the mid-afternoon siesta. One man, apparently homeless, was using a store window to give himself a quick shave. A few people were sitting on the benches, but their backs were to the sea. Their expressionless faces reflected the city's mass of petrified stone as though its citizens slept and watched with both eyes closed. Was the Fata Morgana just one more thing from above that would never lower itself to the depths of this city, or was the city refusing to lift itself off the ground to rise to the height of illusion?

I turned to see if the women were looking out their window. The daughter was repositioning the chicken so her mother could feel the kicks in her belly. I smiled and asked if it was a boy or a girl. She laughed and held up two fingers—maybe one of each.

I wanted to ask them if they came to look for the Fata Morgana, but the mother was now examining the chicken, feeling under its feathers and showing the daughter how she would prepare it for dinner that evening.

They began to gather their belongings. Before they left their seats to exit the bus, I took one last look at the lifeless bird resting on a growing belly, its broken neck draped over the daughter's arm. I couldn't help but think of my mother's and great-grandmother's San Procopio, how different it was from my father's. I wondered if the two worlds would ever meet when we got to their hill town, if I was waiting for the impossible. But as I glanced out the window at the grit of rubbled buildings and water softened by a light mist, it didn't seem strange at all. Maybe because I dare to see through my great-grandmother's eyes, eyes embedded in the stone of memory and the flow of its reinvention.

A story told and retold through the generations: father to daughter, grandfather to granddaughter and on to her children. It rises like a dark mountain that bears witness to family history but whose rock is a castle lit with towers and windows to envision a future. Ours.